"Tonight you're mine."

Tristan was doing everything in his power to keep from tearing off Juliana's clothes and slipping into her. He was hard and ready, had been that way since this afternoon.

But when he'd seen her in that short skirt and those boots?

Harder and readier.

"What's your pleasure, Juliana? We've got hours to do whatever you like." He nuzzled her ear and she gasped.

He reached underneath that short skirt, coaxing his fingers between her legs, where she was already slick against her silk panties. Her readiness thrilled him, stirring him into a light-headed mess of diminishing control. He bent, slid his arm under her knees, picked her up and headed toward the pool, where the waterfall banged away as powerfully as the lust that was driving him.

Then suddenly it hit him. They weren't dabbling in tentative backseat exploration anymore. They were adults—with very real adult needs. He knew it. She knew it.

There was so much more at stake now. Afterward, they would go back to their regular lives, putting their Japanese trip behind them.

But at least they'd have tonight. And Tristan was determined to make sure Juliana never forgot a single, sensual detail....

Dear Reader,

This book reflects my own experience in Japan—
mostly. I didn't do a tour of the "exotic and erotic,"
but the observations you'll read here are culled
from the journal I kept as well as other resources,
such as Liza Dalby's fantastic *Geisha*. And believe
it or not, many elements echo my own adventure
in this wonderful country—things like the guy who
sings "Locomotion" in chapter two and the details
of the snack bar Tristan and Juliana end up visiting.

Yup, those are real, and all of this is a love letter to
Japan.

You can get just a hint of the fun by going to
my Web site at www.crystal-green.com, where I
have a travelogue detailing my trip. Just click on
Crystal's Hyperchick Japan Adventure Part 1 and
Part 2, and you're there!

Hope you enjoy,

Crystal Green
www.crystal-green.com

When the Sun
Goes Down...

CRYSTAL GREEN

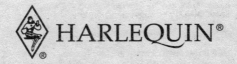

HARLEQUIN®

TORONTO • NEW YORK • LONDON
AMSTERDAM • PARIS • SYDNEY • HAMBURG
STOCKHOLM • ATHENS • TOKYO • MILAN • MADRID
PRAGUE • WARSAW • BUDAPEST • AUCKLAND

Recycling programs
for this product may
not exist in your area.

ISBN-13: 978-0-373-79476-8

WHEN THE SUN GOES DOWN...

www.eHarlequin.com

Printed in U.S.A.

ABOUT THE AUTHOR

Crystal Green lives in Nevada, where she writes Harlequin Blaze novels, Silhouette Special Edition books and vampire tales. She loves to read, overanalyze movies, practice yoga, travel and detail her obsessions on her Web page, www.crystal-green.com. Her trip to Japan was a high point in her life, and you can see much of it on her site in the Hyperchick Adventure section.

Books by Crystal Green

Don't miss any of our special offers. Write to us at the following address for information on our newest releases.

Harlequin Reader Service
U.S.: 3010 Walden Ave., P.O. Box 1325, Buffalo, NY 14269
Canadian: P.O. Box 609, Fort Erie, Ont. L2A 5X3

To Scott and Joy, the host and hostess with the very mostest. You guys are the best.

1

"GOODBYE TO GIRL FRIDAY," Juliana Thomsen said, leaning back on a bench at Atami Harbor and giving in to her jet lag just for a second. The flip-flop time change from California to Japan was finally catching up to her after yesterday's reprieve, and sitting here with her feet in a public foot tub with 113-degree water wasn't doing much to keep her perky.

Her friend and traveling partner, Sasha, tested the water with her fingers and jerked them back. Her strawberry-blond curls fought against the tight ponytail that contained them, but the salt-laced breeze wasn't coaxing even a strand out of place as she gave Juliana a what-are-you-talking-about? glance.

"Girl Friday," Juliana repeated, lifting her own long blond hair off her neck, which was clammy with the early-June humidity. "My family started calling me that when I came back to Parisville to take over the managerial duties in our bookstore after Aunt Katrina decided to retire. Maybe it's just that my life is over there and I'm here, but this trip makes me think I can actually leave all that behind for a while."

Sasha smiled and fixed her gaze on the gleaming water, where boats cut through the blue. "Best of luck then, because that's sure not why your aunt sent you overseas."

Sighing, Juliana took in the decadence of sitting on a boardwalk bench in an exotic country, with its pagodas and koi fish and geisha. Underneath the ornamentation, there was an undercurrent of something hidden—dark alleys under rainfall, neon flickering in the night—and it reflected how she felt about herself, too.

Unexplored.

It had only been on the plane, away from her loving yet majorly attentive family, that freedom had enveloped her.

This would be the perfect time to explore those dark alleys and find something different, something away from the overly interested gaze of the great-aunt who had raised her for the past twenty-four years, since her parents had died in a small-plane crash when she was only eight.

Yet Aunt Katrina was the reason Juliana was even *in* Japan, and she loved the woman who'd become her surrogate mom too much to goof around and let her down.

So, maybe it really would have to be duty before adventure, Juliana thought, preparing herself for the task she'd been sent here to do: securing the painting her family had been chasing for generations—*Dream Rising*, a watercolor that had been lost for over a century.

And an obsession for the elders in the Thomsen family.

A Japanese art dealer named Jiro Mori had uncovered the notorious painting in a Phoenix flea market, then shipped it here with the intention of selling it in his Tokyo gallery. Mori had played hardball, saying he had a lot of business in Japan and couldn't make it to the west coast of America for another month, so when his phone negotiations with Aunt Katrina had gone bust, the canny woman, the historian of the family, had put Juliana on a plane. The elder Thomsen thought that her great-niece, with her "persuasive blond good looks and head for business," might be able to negotiate more effectively in person—before it was too late.

In other words, before the Coles, the family who'd also been tracking the painting, found its location.

As Juliana stared at her painted toenails under the hot water, her heart clutched, her belly swirled, and her gaze blurred into a different image altogether—a memory of a sketch she'd seen of *Dream Rising*.

Misty curves and entwined limbs. Out of the tangles, a woman, her hair loose, her body explicitly bared and vulnerable, seemed to rise, reaching for something just beyond her grasp.

Juliana had first seen the sketch when she was nine, after her parents' deaths, after she'd drawn into herself in her grief. In an attempt to help, Aunt Katrina had told her stories about the watercolor—how, generations ago, Terrence Cole, the artist, and his model Emelie, Juliana's great-great-grandmother, had once loved each other. How he'd painted her and captured their affection.

It had only been years later that Juliana had heard the rest: the couple's love had imploded when Terrence had been pressured by his family into an arranged marriage, and he'd asked Emelie to be his mistress.

She'd refused, and that's how the feud between the Thomsens and Coles had started; when Emelie and Terrence had broken apart generations ago, she had thought that *Dream Rising* had been his sentimental farewell gift to her, and he had insisted that it wasn't. When she'd reported the painting as stolen, a bitterness had been born, morphing through the years into disagreements between the two families about such things as disputed property lines between the Coles' ranch and the Thomsens' land, opposing views of political matters in Parisville, a car accident that had injured one Thomsen while the Cole party had gotten off scot-free.

It never seemed to end.

Once, Juliana had almost challenged the feud.

Once.

Those misty colors of the painting kept weaving through her mind as she recalled how she and Tristan Cole had come so close to falling in love after high school, just before she'd left for college. But they hadn't found the courage to go all the way, either in the backseat of his vintage Mustang or by shouting out how they'd felt about each other to the world.

If they had, hell would've rained down, and they'd both known it. You just didn't talk to members of the other family if you ran into them at the market or coffee shop. You pretended to look the other way in the school hallways, even if someone as breathtaking as Tristan, with his longish black hair and mysterious gaze, walked on by.

Juliana had nursed a quiet crush on him for years, starting in grade school, flowering in junior high, then coming to a head in senior year. And one summer's night, she'd found out that he'd felt the same, watching her as she'd watched him without either of them realizing it.

But they'd been too young, she thought as her gaze solidified once again, the water, the rocks beneath her feet wavering under her vision. They hadn't been mature enough to handle the consequences, and she'd chosen to go off to college, to a different world, never forgetting what could've been with the boy who'd always sat at the back of the class, dangerous and quiet.

Yet she'd lived plenty of years without Tristan. She hadn't even seen him around their small, inland town because he kept to himself in his cabin on the family ranch property, no doubt locked away in that garage of his, working on those vintage cars he'd always loved. Parisville, with its pines and nearby mountains, was big enough these days that there were unfamiliar people crowding the streets, yet quaint enough that even a feud could still separate a could've-been couple.

She often caught herself wondering just what she'd missed out on with Tristan....

Sasha nudged Juliana, whose heart sank at the loss of the memory.

"Should we start heading out now?" her friend asked.

Juliana exhaled, dizzy from not breathing while she was woolgathering. Lethargic from the water's heat, too. "We could go to my meeting, I suppose."

"Good." Sasha stood and stretched. "You know, even though your art-dealer guy messed up, we'll reap some benefits."

They'd scheduled a meeting at his Tokyo gallery but Jiro Mori had changed the location at the last minute because he had sudden business with an artist in Atami.

Juliana rose, also. "It was decent of him to give us train tickets to get here. Besides, Atami wasn't a ridiculously long ride from our hotel."

"This town's an intriguing place. A gem, really," Sasha said. "On the train, I was reading that Atami literally means *hot sea* because of the volcano-heated water. And this whole faded hot-spring resort vibe adds... I don't know. Character. Sadness." She paused. "The *shogun* were supposed to have taken the waters here, and during its heyday, a sort of side industry was built around the area to attract more tourists. That's why we've got things like adult museums and '*onsen* geisha' to check in to here."

Juliana's interest was piqued; she'd spent her life curious about everyone else on the planet. "*Onsen* means *hot springs,* right? I haven't read about the difference between a 'hot-springs geisha' and any other."

"They go against the traditional standard and offer sex rather than wittiness or artistic entertainment, as opposed to what you'd find in the more refined districts like, say, Gion." Sasha tapped her head. "Can I retain the info or what?"

"You certainly can."

So...Atami. Maybe it'd be the perfect place for Juliana to start peeking into some of those dark alleys she'd been thinking about.

She happily splashed some water out of the foot tub as she and Sasha got out. What if she enlisted her partner in hopeful crime for some Atami adventuring? After all, she'd been able to persuade Sasha, who'd been a great friend since she'd moved to Parisville last spring to live with her boyfriend—a Cole, as a matter of fact—to come along to Japan in the first place.

Since Sasha had left Parisville recently, they hadn't seen much of each other, even though they still gabbed on the phone all the time. And maybe Juliana was just a little rebellious; Aunt Katrina and the family had never been crazy about Juliana's relationship with Sasha, the "Cole moll." She didn't want to lose this friendship. A travel author, Sasha loved to read just as much as Juliana did, and fed her friend's adventurous streak with stories of her road trips throughout the U.S. Sasha seemed to have it all so together, while Juliana, herself, didn't.

Juliana had also invited Sasha on this trip because she'd been skittish about coming alone to this country, with all its complicated customs and a language she couldn't even begin to understand. Heck, she hadn't even left the States before, so she figured Sasha, with all her travel experience as a single girl, would be excellent company.

Even if *she'd* never been to Japan, either.

They dried off, put on their sandals, rolling down their pant legs before returning their gratis towels, then bowing in deference to the little old woman who'd summoned them over to the foot baths in the first place.

Afterward, they continued their strolling along the boardwalk in the direction of the ramen house where Juliana was scheduled to meet Jiro Mori, passing ice-cream vendors who peddled their wares under Atami Castle, which loomed on a hill above it all. The castle was a gray-and-white pagoda that peered from a cluster of mountaintop trees; a ropeway strung up the inclined path seemed to attach the past with the boardwalk's concession-cart present.

"You're going to check out that art exhibition at the castle during my lunch?" Juliana asked, tilting her face back to the sunshine.

It warmed her in the chill aftermath of those memories of Tristan. She couldn't seem to shake them after unearthing feelings left buried for years.

Sasha held up her big purse, which contained her trusty notebook, digital camera and audio recorder. "Castle-bound, that's me."

Laughing, Juliana was careful to keep her voice down. "You know, there's a yummy irony about you, of all people, coming with me to research a book about hot adventures in Japan."

"Hmm. Somehow I recall that you suggested I come along. Or maybe a better way to say it is you *begged* me."

"I didn't beg. No begging. I just knew that you were looking for a hot topic, and I put a bug in your ear. *The Exotic and Erotic: Beyond the Kimono.*" Juliana grinned at her friend mischievously. "I still think that's the title you should go with."

"Anything that'll get this book flying off the shelves."

"Hey, doubting yourself isn't allowed. When you pitched this idea to your editor, she ate it up."

Sasha sighed. "I just hope I'm not being impulsive, jumping the gun before going to contract. This trip is costing a pretty penny."

Juliana knew that Sasha used to live comfortably on her stock dividends, but these days there were no guarantees. Having another successful product on the shelves was important to her, especially since she had published only two modestly successful travel-based books already.

"Okay," Sasha added, responding to Juliana's lingering look. "Maybe I'm also nervous because of the subject matter. I mean, you want to read about a jaunt in California's northern wine region? I'm your scribe. Want to explore U.S. cowboy country? Look me up. But uncovering the not-as-obvious exotic and erotic here in a place that a lot of Americans look at as being repressed and buttoned-down?"

"It'll be fun."

"Just remember," Sasha said, sending Juliana a lowered glance. "As soon as your family business is taken care of, you're going to be there step by step with me, checking out the love hotels, geisha and sexy bars. And we've got to try the hot springs here."

"I did promise." And Juliana had decided to make the most of it, too.

To embrace something different. Something exciting that she hadn't felt since high school...

For discretion's sake, Juliana took a gander around, checking that they were far enough away from anyone on the boardwalk to chat openly. During her rushed studies for this trip, she'd read that the Japanese were generally educated in English, and she didn't want to sound like a loudmouth *gaijin,* or foreigner. Truth was, she and Sasha stood out enough with their light hair and skin—things that had seemed to garner some notice on the trains they'd taken from Tokyo this morning. If there was one thing Juliana had learned so far, it was that the citizens were friendly and welcoming, yet there was a bold, thick line between visiting and actually *belonging* to a country where there was such great pride in being Japanese.

The adults were subtle in their curiosity about foreigners, but the children stared at them before their parents corrected their behavior. However, neither Juliana nor Sasha had been embarrassed about the attention, even though being watched was something to get used to; in Parisville, there were a lot of blond people running around, so Juliana had never realized that she could stick out like a sore thumb.

Hmm...

Being watched, she thought, her mind going to naughty places. If she could find a voyeur here—a tall, dark-haired man with intense gray eyes...

A jag of lust twisted inside her.

Juliana lowered her voice. "You think we'll find any adventures here in Atami? I mean, besides your cheeky art exhibit?"

"Just listen to *you.* Didn't you get enough adventure before you moved back, living out of town?"

A pang traveled through Juliana. She missed residing in San Diego, where, after college, she'd moved to help found a company that put together private, eclectic tours of downtown. With all the tales of Wyatt Earp and tragic gas-lamp romances the job had spoken to Juliana's creative, whimsical side. But then she'd been asked to take over the family bookstore, the pride of her aunt Katrina, which did constant business with its attached cheesecake-and-coffee café.

She hadn't been able to refuse the relative who'd given so much for her, so she'd sold her portion of the tour business and returned to Parisville.

Sacrifice for sacrifice, she thought. *Quid pro quo.*

"I haven't had an adventure in a while," Juliana admitted to Sasha. "Frankly, these days, I don't even date within the limits of Parisville—not if I want to avoid being given the third degree. My family still probably thinks I'm a nice girl."

"Little do they know."

Juliana shrugged. She'd had her share of dates during her

years of freedom, none of them leading to any serious commitment. And none of them had gotten her *there,* in her heart.

Or in the part of her that longed for the explosive romance the stories of Emelie and Terrence, while they'd still been in love, had led her to expect.

Call her an idealist, but she'd been holding out for something epic.

"And you?" Juliana asked. "How far do you want to go with your own personal research?"

"Not that far."

Even now, almost a year after the breakup that'd persuaded Sasha to leave Parisville, Juliana could see the pain on her friend's face.

And why not? Chad Cole had broken Sasha's heart by refusing to acknowledge that her dreams and goals were as important as his. They'd split up because he'd gotten more and more possessive of her time, it had come to a head when he'd pretty much given her an ultimatum—her career or him.

Sasha had chosen the career, thinking that the problem went beyond just this one issue, and she'd moved to Orange County, over an hour away from Chad and Parisville.

"Chad was a long time ago," Juliana said. "You're allowed to have fun with men now. The mourning period has come and gone."

"I do. Have fun, I mean."

Juliana didn't have the heart to contradict her. "Chad Cole is old, old news, Sash. *This* is our future—a rollicking good time in a place where no one will gossip about us behind our backs. If you're naughty in Atami, I won't tell a soul."

For a second, Sasha's deep-blue eyes lit up with hope. Yes, they were here, unleashed from the past and present, weren't they?

But then a young Japanese couple walked by, laughing with each other, licking their ice-cream cones.

Sasha's gaze lost its sparkle, and suddenly, to Juliana, this trip became about much more than just a watercolor or Sasha's newest book—it was about putting that hope back in her friend's gaze.

But Sasha's mind was obviously still on Chad, even though she had a roundabout way of mentioning him.

"Have you thought of what bringing home that watercolor is going to do to the Coles?" she asked.

"I expect their family will be pretty unhappy about it since they've been after the piece for all these years, too. That's why the old-school Thomsen crowd funded this trip for me, you know—so they could parade the symbolic object of their moral victory over the Coles up and down Main Street, daring them to say something, *anything* about how one person supposedly stole the painting from another and just look who's got a hold of it now. I'm just their tool."

"Hardly a tool," Sasha said.

They smiled at each other.

"Have I ever told you," Juliana said, "that I'm glad we got to be friends even though you were with one of *them?*"

Sasha gave her a tiny, yet affectionate, bump.

They stopped on the boardwalk, ready to go their separate ways.

"Are you sure you don't want me to go with you?" Sasha asked.

"No, you've got your sexy research to do. Besides, I've already chatted with Jiro Mori on the phone, so I know he's one of these young guys who's into Western culture. Communication's been easy because his English is great." She laughed. "I won't be needing you as a crutch for the time being."

"Maybe I'll need *you*. There aren't many signs in English around here."

Sasha's smile told Juliana that she was kidding.

"All right then," Juliana said. "You do your thing and I'll call you when my appointment ends. It'll probably be about two hours until we can meet up." They'd rented cell phones with international calling plans. Expensive, but worth it. "Then after we check into those hot baths, we'll train it back to Tokyo and get into trouble in the Roppongi District tonight."

Nightclubs, cabarets… A good start to see what else they could find.

"Okay," her friend said. "So let's meet by the entrance to the Adult Museum near the castle when you're done? You might get a kick out of the displays."

"Sounds like a plan."

As they parted ways, Juliana did feel a little cautious about continuing on her own, but it wasn't because Japan was dangerous. Far from it.

There was just something about setting out solo, Juliana thought while taking her first step into this looking-glass world that was so different from the one she was used to.

But Juliana was starting to believe that she actually might have the strength to find her own way here, far away from home.

Far away from the woman everyone else expected her to be.

WHEN TRISTAN COLE saw Juliana Thomsen lingering in front of a seafood stand in the cluttered, tempura-scented alley that led to the ramen house where he was scheduled to meet Jiro Mori, he stopped in his tracks.

The ecstatic shock of seeing her again made his body clutch up with the memories that were resurfacing.

A summer night just before Juliana was set to go off to Cal Poly. A bonfire out in Taggert's Field, the hills casting shadows while dusk settled.

He'd been drinking a beer, just like the other underage kids, when the conversation had faded to whispers.

When he'd glanced away from his lone spot at the fire to see why, he'd found her, surrounded by friends—good girls who'd braved the party as a lark before going off to their new lives.

His gaze had connected with hers, then held and, now, he remembered how his gut had tightened, blood rushing to his groin and his head as his secret fantasy had stared right back at him over the flames.

The crush he'd never talked about or acted on.

He'd waited until she was away from her buddies, then while she was passing a tree that he stood against away from the rest of the party, he'd spoken to her for the first time ever.

She'd stopped, lingered, and he could see that she was interested, the violet of her eyes shining in the moonlight.

Later, after they'd small-talked for as long as he could take, he'd reached out, brought her against his body, leaned back against the rough tree and kissed her.

And for one secret, stolen week, they'd kissed some more. More. Until that one night, when they'd come so close....

He'd ached to be inside her, ached afterward when they'd decided that their families would never understand if they went any further.

Then she'd left town, making him wonder if she'd been relieved to do so, if she'd only been experimenting with him and now that it was done, she was content.

But as for him?

Long afterward, he'd wondered if she'd been the one who'd gotten away, and based on his romantic experiences ever since, he was just about convinced that nobody would ever come close to Juliana Thomsen.

Now she was here, in Japan, the last place he'd ever expected.

He smiled tightly. He'd been pulled in to this drama by his cousin and the rest of his family, who'd enlisted him to chase down *Dream Rising,* the painting the Cole family had coveted for years. The piece that would finally stick it to the Thomsens and give some closure to the whole damned Terrence/Emelie legend.

But it was also the object that would give Gramps Cole the pride he'd been searching for in his waning days. In an effort not to feel "old and useless"—a phrase he often bandied about, much to Tristan's dismay—Gramps had put it upon himself to find the painting, but time after time, his ego had been beaten down by failure. As well, he had taken personally his loss in a dispute over some property lines between the two families.

If the painting was all it would take to give his grandfather some pride back, Tristan was going to get it for him.

He'd been chosen to do this family errand mostly because he'd taken some Japanese; in reality, he'd only listened to a few learn-on-your-own language tapes because he did business with a certain car nut over here—one of many clients who kept Tristan flush with cash from hunting down vintage finds for collectors of American automobiles. But Gramps had figured Tristan would be a good candidate to accompany Chad.

"I'd go on the trip myself," the old man had said softly from his bed, "but these damned legs won't carry me. Do your dad proud, Tristan. He would have asked you to go if he were still alive."

Tristan's mom had stayed quiet during the entire meeting, watching her son, who'd so far done well at staying out of family politics, get sucked right in.

He'd just never felt a part of their *Dream Rising* feud. Hell, he hadn't even felt much affinity for their horse-breeding business, either, preferring to spend most of his time under a car hood.

But he'd do anything for Gramps, so that's why he was standing here in this alley, moving aside for the foot traffic to pass.

Next to him, Chad was watching Juliana Thomsen, too, but not for the same reason as Tristan.

"She's here to meet Jiro Mori," his cousin said, having no idea about what had happened between Tristan and Juliana so long ago.

"Makes sense," Tristan answered casually. "Both our families have been tracking that painting, so it stands to reason that the art dealer would make the most of a competing interest in it. Smart businessman, if you ask me. He must sense that whoever gets their hands on it will be the winner after all these years of skirmishing."

He could feel Chad's considering gaze on him, but his attention was drawn back to Juliana and her shimmer of silky hair that seemed to weave both silver and gold down her back. He knew her eyes would still be that hue he'd never seen except in old-movie Technicolor. Violet.

Just picturing what she was going to look like when she fully turned around—an adult, over fourteen years after they'd been so close to really being with each other—got his libido running harder.

"What's with you?" Chad asked, his wire-rimmed glasses making him come off like a professor.

"Just enjoying the sights."

His cousin went silent. Chad was appeasing the elders of the family just as much as Tristan; his job was to expedite the financing. Not that the family was rich, but they had squirreled away a lot of money over the years in the hope of finding the holy grail of Terrence's paintings, and Chad was the family accountant, the purse strings. It'd be up to Tristan and his so-called experience with overseas clients to negotiate while his cousin waited in the background.

Tristan had resigned himself to the whole thing and just wanted to get it over with so he could enjoy himself somewhat. He'd told himself that coming to Japan was a gift in disguise, because he could meet his biggest car patron face-to-face for the first time. It'd be good business.

Yet he found his gaze drawn back to Juliana Thomsen as she accepted a sample of grilled octopus from a fishmonger.

Octopus, he thought. An aphrodisiac.

She looked around at the paper lanterns hanging over the alley while she chewed, as if she was thoroughly enjoying her surroundings, the excitement of it all.

He glanced at Chad, then back at Juliana. They weren't in Parisville. Why not get closer?

He started to move down the alley toward her, his blood simmering, making him go a little light-headed, a little more careless than the silent guy who always kept to himself.

He could hear Chad following as Juliana bowed to the fishmonger, then started to leave...

Only to turn around and find Tristan blocking her way.

She took a step back, sucking in a breath, her eyes wide.

As she stared at him, clearly thrown by the idea that he was here in the same country, the same alley, the violet of her eyes mesmerized him, and he could've sworn that he detected something there.

Happiness at seeing him again?

Wonder about what could've been between them?

Or was she a full Thomsen by now, having left behind all the girlish ideals she'd possessed back when they'd laid a blanket over the backseat of his car and slowly, agonizingly peeled the clothes off each other? As they'd found themselves in the throes of what he'd naively thought could've turned into love?

She swallowed, then laughed slightly while glancing

at Chad, too. He knew she was recovering, just as he was still doing.

"This shouldn't stun me," she said, a barely perceptible tremor in her voice. "I suppose whoever's been charged with keeping track of *Dream Rising* in your family got the same lead we did."

He couldn't help coasting a longer look over her. When she noticed, her fair skin—which already seemed as if it'd gotten some sun—went even pinker.

Chad's voice edged into the tension. "You're brave, Ms. Thomsen. Coming overseas alone to take care of business."

She dragged her gaze away from Tristan's, and all he wanted to do was drag it back.

"I'm with a friend," she said to Chad. "And I suppose I should put this out there so there're no more surprises—it's Sasha."

Chad didn't say anything for a moment, and Tristan thought that might be because the wind had been knocked out of his heart-on-the-sleeve-wearing cousin.

Poor guy. Tristan knew the details of the failed romance; over many a brew, Chad had revealed his regret at becoming too territorial with her. He'd only loved her, he'd said. He'd learned a lot over the months since their breakup, but he couldn't imagine Sasha ever taking him back.

Standing here with Juliana, Tristan realized that he felt just like Chad looked. Hollow. Hell, Tristan had been feeling empty for a while.

What would his life have been like if he and Juliana had only been brave enough to tell their families where to stick their feud? At eighteen, she hadn't wanted to, and he'd understood, because living a life as a black sheep hadn't appealed to him, either. Not when he loved his family the way he did.

Juliana was measuring Chad's reaction to the news of Sasha; she was obviously on guard for her friend, and that gave Tristan the opportunity to take her in again, to think about how fresh, wide-eyed and still somehow innocent she was after the passage of all these years.

Chad finally replied, "Can you tell me where Sasha is?"

Good God, man, Tristan thought. *Take it back.*

Juliana narrowed her eyes, as if she regretted revealing Sasha's presence. But then she sighed, probably realizing that they were all adults here and she had no reason to be a hard case about this.

"She went to the art exhibition at Atami Castle," she said. "Research for a book she's writing."

But even that wasn't enough for Chad. "How is she?"

"Chad," Tristan said in warning.

The other man seemed to take the caution into account, but then he sent a lopsided, sheepish grin to Tristan. It was a gesture announcing that he'd wanted to see Sasha again ever since the night she'd left him. A smile that admitted he'd never stopped carrying a torch for her and would be damned if, after all this time regretting it, he would let an opportunity like this go by.

Tristan almost took a step back at that thought.

A second chance. Here, in Japan, where no one might ever know...

Chad started to leave. "Call me when you're done?" he said to Tristan.

Juliana looked as if she wanted to stop him, too, but as Chad merged with the walking traffic, neither of them said anything to bring him back.

They only watched him go, his sandy head visible above the other dark, bobbing ones until he disappeared around a corner.

"Well," he heard Juliana say. "I suppose I'll see you in the ramen house with Jiro Mori then."

He turned around to find her already walking away and trying to access her cell phone, as if to call Sasha. When it looked like the reception wasn't cooperating, she put the phone into her purse and took out a paper, then scanned the shops around her.

Probably her own set of directions from Jiro Mori, Tristan thought, while enjoying the smooth curve of her rear under her skirt. He also couldn't help reveling in the swish of her straight hair teasing the middle of her back because he remembered how soft it'd been when he'd sifted his fingers through it.

He caught up to her with his long strides. "Chad's not going to make a menace of himself, if that's what you're afraid of."

"I know," Juliana said. "And why wouldn't he try to talk with Sasha? It's been months. They've both had some distance from what happened, so they'll be civil."

The past kept a cushion between them, and all he wanted to do was poke it by saying what was really on his mind.

But maybe he should ease into it.

"Civil." The word seemed as foreign as they were. "Somehow, it doesn't seem like *civil* should belong in a conversation between a Cole and a Thomsen."

She kept walking, but at a slower pace, slow enough that he could smell her flowery shampoo, her warm skin under the humidity.

A shiver skated up his flesh, rolling out. God, she smelled the same, and he realized that he'd imagined that scent many, many times over the years, but somehow, it had remained elusive.

How elusive was it now, though? he wondered.

"I'll be honest," she said. "I've never been very attached to this whole *Dream Rising* history. I'm here for the yakitori and sake."

He lifted a brow.

She laughed. "I came for my aunt Katrina. She and my other aunts and uncles have their hearts set on this painting. I just want to secure it, then have a little amusement before I head back home."

"Unless *I* get the painting for the Coles."

She came to a gradual stop, glancing up at him. But what he thought might be a challenging look turned to something softer, her eyes filling with the same memories he couldn't let go of, either.

His body responded with even more force this time, a growing erection pressing against his fly. Teenage lust, he thought. It had never died.

That's all it was.

He focused on her mouth. It was enough to distract anyone all on its own, with the way it turned down at the tips, giving her a lush, slightly pouty look that played well with the vivid flash of her eyes.

"Okay," he said, "I'll be honest, too. I'm here because of Gramps, for the most part. He's getting on in years and..."

"You just want to see him happy."

Both of them were silent, the air between them thick and hot. His gaze lingered on her mouth, and he tasted her kisses again.

He'd never forgotten, and it just took seeing her once more to realize it.

She bit her lip, obviously having caught his appreciation of it, and her mouth shaped into a tentative smile that scrambled his brain.

But his body read things loud and clear. She was just as attracted as he was—there was something steaming up her imagination with the same humid condensation fogging his.

Then she began walking again, slower now. "I guess it'd be great revenge for whoever ends up with the painting."

"'There is more real pleasure to be gotten out of a malicious act, where your heart is in it, than out of thirty acts of a nobler sort,'" he said.

She smiled, almost to herself, probably remembering his habit of quoting Mark Twain, his father's favorite author. His dad had read *Tom Sawyer* and *Huckleberry Finn* to Tristan most nights of grade school, and Juliana, who'd always been a brainiac, even before taking over the cheesecake-and-book store recently, would know her Twain.

She laughed, and the sound soothed through him, mixing with the heat. But instead of cooling him off, his lust burned higher.

He came to her side. As if by accident, her shoulder brushed his arm.

White heat jolted him.

Her voice seemed choked when she finally said, "In spite of the circumstances, it's good to see you again, Tristan."

His name on her lips.

"It's good to see you again, too," he said, wishing he could say more, but wary about doing so.

After all, she'd left him and never came back. What they'd had couldn't have meant all that much to her.

He decided to exact his own little revenge by brushing against *her*.

Friction seemed to spark between them.

He thought he heard her take in a quick breath, the ensuing rhythm of it matching his own escalating heart-beat.

As if in agreement, they came to a halt in front of the ramen house, and with a secretive smile, she winged by him once more, her hand skimming his hand in a subtle, yet earth-rocking move.

His vision blanked—a zap of electricity that sizzled on a wire through the rest of his body, from his fingers to his gut.

As she entered the restaurant, he stayed outside, gathering himself.

Preparing to take up where the woman he shouldn't want had left him all those years ago.

2

WHEN JULIANA ENTERED the ramen house, fully aware that Tristan had yet to follow, she could still feel him on her flesh: heavy and musky. He'd gotten *under* her skin, too—a rushing heat that was injecting her with need.

At first she told herself that she was just in shock from seeing him here, and that had muddled her mind. But how did it explain the dampness between her legs, the quiver in her belly?

Dark alleys, she thought. Exploration.

She was away from home, in a world where no one knew her, where she didn't even quite feel like herself. And there Tristan had been in the alley, watching her from a heated distance just as he had the first night they'd kissed.

A sharp yearning consumed her. Regret.

How many times had she wondered what he would have felt like inside her? How they would have moved together as the radio had played slow, languorous songs in the sanctuary of his car?

But, now, just like back then, she thought of the family, and how they would consider what she was feeling a betrayal.

Even so, tingles consumed her as she tried to clear her mind by glancing around the small, slim eatery, which featured booths, a long counter and woven rice paper decorating the walls. The employees, who were busy behind the counter, bowed and said, *"Irasshaimase,"* greeting her, and she smiled and bowed back to them. A young Japanese man wearing dark-framed glasses and a shirt with a peace symbol waved to her from his counter seat. He was drinking a bottle of beer, but from the way he kept grinning and grinning, she thought he might have had a lot more than just one.

It felt a bit isolated in here, she thought. Another world away from the one outside.

Then she saw a twentysomething man who might be her art dealer, Jiro Mori, in a booth tucked into the back corner. She made her way toward him.

Even though he had his head down, madly scribbling into a notebook—running numbers based on how much he could make from this sale?—she saw the blue streaks in his shag-cut hair and the paisley long-sleeved shirt. He definitely matched the description he'd given her over the phone.

She kept her distance from the table, waiting for an opportune moment to greet him, but he didn't notice her, and she respected his peace, thinking it might be considered rude to interrupt.

All the while, her flesh danced with the anticipation of Tristan's entrance; with one glance back at the door, she found that he still hadn't come in.

Had that last little brush against him gotten to him as much as it'd gotten to her? Or was he taking a break from her because she'd gone too far in a country where public displays of affection weren't kosher?

She wouldn't blame him for wanting to keep a few feet between him and her. He'd been just as adamant about respecting his family's feelings back then as she had, and that's why she'd gone off to college without ever giving in to her desires, even though they'd haunted her long afterward.

No one had ever kissed her or touched her as he had.

No one had even gotten close.

She wiped the back of her neck. Sweaty, she thought, and not just from the weather.

Juliana realized that the young man at the counter was talking to her, so she listened as he rattled off a string of words that she couldn't understand.

She took her phrase book out of her purse and found the right page. *"Nihongo wa wakarimasen."*

I don't understand Japanese.

He said whatever he was saying slower. She heard the word *English* in there and nodded.

Then he started singing "The Locomotion" to her until the older man and woman behind the counter interrupted with their own blast of Japanese. It sounded like they weren't happy with him.

She heard Jiro stir behind her, and when she faced him, she saw he'd gotten out of the booth and was holding out a hand to shake instead of the usual bowing.

Westernized, she thought. When she'd done some Internet research on his Tokyo gallery, which did a lot of business with foreigners, she saw that he spent a lot of time jet-setting in Europe.

"Miss Thomsen?" he asked.

"Yes."

"Thank you for changing plans and meeting me here instead of Tokyo."

"Thank you for inviting me, Mr. Mori."

They shook hands, and he led her to one side of the booth. "I'm afraid I was in my own world a few moments ago," he said. "So sorry."

She wasn't sure just *how* Westernized he was, so she went ahead with what she'd discovered in her travel research and told him that she'd be presenting him with a gift—expensive candies that she'd purchased at a shop in her hotel.

She hoped she was doing this right, because like most other things in Japan, gift-giving had its list of do's and don'ts.

All these cultural land mines, she thought. They'd keep her on her toes.

And so would Tristan, she couldn't help adding, a wave of sensation whisking through her.

Jiro Mori laughed, thanked her and sat opposite her in the booth. "You're nervous, I can see that. But you're doing fine, Miss Thomsen. Japan's quite a place for foreigners to negotiate."

"Tougher than any place I've been before, that's for sure." Armchair-traveling and exploring San Diego's nooks and crannies for the purpose of her old business had been her substitute for all the world traveling she'd thought she'd do once upon a time.

Again, she wondered where Tristan was. At the thought of him her heart jumped, her belly curled, her sex throbbed, and she glanced over her shoulder, still waiting for him to walk through that door and stun her senseless again.

Jiro Mori obviously thought she was keeping tabs on the tipsy guy at the counter. The owners clearly believed so, too, because they began scolding "The Locomotion" dude again.

"They're telling him not to embarrass their country," Jiro said, sotto voce.

But then a flood of awareness cascaded down her body, and before Jiro even began to rise out of the booth, she knew that Tristan had finally entered.

When he arrived at the table, she tried not to look at him. But she was sharply tuned in to his scent, bay leaves—how that took her back—as he and the art dealer went through the same greeting-and-gift scene.

All the while, she couldn't deny that her skin had turned into a live playground for goose bumps, and the tingling between her legs grew stronger.

In spite of herself, she ended up taking a peek at him.

From an eighteen-year-old to a man.

And what a man: handsome, with his black hair still longish, slouching over his brow with badass carelessness. But his gray eyes gleamed even in the midst of a certain cloudiness. He had such angles to his face, too: sloping cheekbones, a firm jawline. Strength and beauty and a quiet confidence that had always done something to her and had never been replicated.

As Jiro moved to the counter and addressed the servers in Japanese, Tristan slid into the booth next to Juliana, a barely there smile tilting his lips.

He was close.

Real close.

His muscled forearm whisked against hers, and her heart slapped against her breastbone.

She took a breath, knowing her family would be up in arms if they were here to see them.

But they weren't, Juliana thought. It was just the two of them.

Her sense of freedom expanded, consuming her.

"Took long enough for your grand entrance," she said in a low voice as Jiro carried on his conversation with the servers.

"Had to cool off a little out there, seeing as I imagined it might get hotter in here." He raised a dark brow. "With negotiations for that painting, I mean."

Under the cover of the table, he put his hand between them on the seat.

His fingers were less than an inch away from her leg, and she swore she felt the pressure of them even at that whisper-thin distance.

Her clit pounded, and she hardly even heard Jiro ask them what they wanted to drink. Then, while the art dealer ordered, Tristan caught her eye.

He was smiling playfully.

And before she knew what he was up to, he ran a finger along the crease of her skirt.

She closed her eyes, suppressed emotion and need hitting her all at once.

Then she heard his voice, soft, whispered.

"Have you ever wondered, Juliana?"

He didn't need to explain, and on a rush of impulse, she found herself saying, "Yes."

When she opened her eyes, their gazes met, his a burning silver, colored with such a passion that she couldn't fight it.

His voice lowered even more. "Have you ever thought of finishing what we started that last night we were together?"

Her vision went dreamlike as she absorbed him.

How many times had she filled in the blanks of that last night, when they'd decided not to go all the way?

But he was asking her to…

Oh, my God. Was he asking her to pretend as if they were still teens and fulfill her most frequent fantasies?

Before she could stop herself, she heard a soft "Yes" repeated from her lips.

He grinned, and she almost slid to the floor in one massive flow.

Then their host's voice interrupted them, and she startled as Jiro Mori sat down.

"Are you enjoying Japan so far?" he asked.

To Juliana, it sounded as if he was talking Swahili in an echo chamber.

She'd told Tristan yes without thinking about it.

And, for once, she was ecstatic to have been so rash.

She managed to talk. "It's beautiful here."

"You find something you didn't expect around every corner," Tristan added.

One of the servers came to their table, setting down a tray with *oshibori*—a hot towel for each of them.

She straightened in her seat, took a towel and wiped her hands, just as the others were doing. It was a pre-meal regularity in this country, one that made Juliana's already-sensitized skin reawaken.

She fought the electric sensation as the server pre-sented Tristan with a bottle of Asahi and her with the makings of a grapefruit sawa, a fresh drink she'd read about. Jiro chatted in Japanese with the woman and, during the distraction, Tristan touched her leg again.

Stifling a gasp, she shifted. She'd said yes, but there was still business to deal with right now.

Damn business.

He moved, too, as if merely to readjust his sitting po-sition. Yet he was really camouflaging his antics under the table as he kept skimming his fingertips along her leg.

A tightness forced her to cross one thigh over the other, which put her out of range of his hand.

He smiled, then reclined, resting his arm on the back of the booth, just behind her, where she could feel the hum of his skin.

She wanted him to touch her again. Coy brushes over the leg weren't enough.

As the server left the table, she couldn't think of any-thing else but her throbbing sex, the dampness that was slicking her undies.

A clueless Jiro gestured to Juliana's beverage, which had been served with a half grapefruit. "You juice your own fruit and add it to the drink mix."

So he thought she wasn't moving because she didn't know what to do with the sawa. Okay, she'd go with that.

She picked up the fruit, noting the irony of having to juice it when the same had been done to her by Tristan.

"So, Mr. Mori," he said, all business *now*. "We have a painting to discuss."

"Direct and to the point." Jiro took a swig of beer, then

swallowed. "I like how you conduct business. And I apologize for not notifying you both about having invited the other party, but I had intended to deal with you separately, and today's little emergency with my associate changed matters. My mind escaped me in the rush." He put down his beer. "Artists can be quite difficult, especially when their work is in demand."

From the way he said it, Juliana thought that maybe Jiro had actually set up this surprise meeting to cause tension between the two interested families, and to whet their appetites for competing for the painting.

No dummy, this guy, she thought.

Nonetheless, both she and Tristan acknowledged their host's apology, and he continued.

"If you don't mind, I wonder if you would indulge me in providing the background on the work first. *Dream Rising* has a scandalous history, and here I have the ancestors of the main players right in front of me."

Okay, so he had an honest enjoyment of gossip. Sounded familiar, except the people in Parisville probably wouldn't admit to their own need for it.

Juliana looked at Tristan, then said lightly, "History says that the painting was lost over a hundred years ago, but that's only part of the truth."

Tristan's mouth quirked in a half grin—a spark to add to what was already crackling between them.

"My great-great-grandfather, Terrence Cole, was the artist," he said. "His subject was…"

He paused, but Juliana could finish. Tristan was probably wondering if saying *his jilted mistress* was acceptable in this company. Even though she'd read that extramarital affairs were commonplace in Japan, he was probably playing the good traveler by not being brash about it.

She decided to throw him a lifeline. "Terrence's subject was my great-great-grandmother, Emelie."

But somehow that didn't seem adequate. Terrence had tossed Emelie out of his life just before he'd married the woman to whom he'd been promised for years. He'd devastated Emelie, and she'd never recovered—not even when she'd married a much, much older German immigrant who'd done well in the gold rush years earlier.

Terrence the heartbreaker.

Jiro nodded. "The story is that she stole the painting, and this set into motion a disagreement between your families that has lasted for a few generations now, yes?"

"You've got it," Juliana said, raising her eyebrows at Tristan.

He waited a beat, just as if he knew she was remembering his fingers on her thigh and how she wished he would have traveled them up and up...

She squeezed her legs together, alleviating a little of the almost painful pleasure.

"We're terrible enemies," Tristan finally said.

His voice was low, rippling through her as she remembered the night they'd decided to let go, never to tell a soul how close they'd come to making love and changing everything.

He removed his arm from the back of the booth and rested his hand on the seat again. Juliana's skin flared, waiting, *hoping* he'd touch her.

But he didn't.

Jiro pursued the subject. "I also heard a rumor that Emelie saw this whole situation quite differently."

"That's true, too." Juliana laid her hand on her purse, where she carried copies of Emelie's letters to her sister. "When Terrence and Emelie parted ways, she found it appropriate to take the painting with her. It was a gift. Then came the accusations, the scandal… But she never returned the watercolor because it was stolen from her own home by an intruder."

"But," Tristan said, "Terrence's diaries say that when he broke off their affair, she got angry and made off with the painting. It wasn't a gift at all."

"And Emelie's letters say that she thought Terrence wanted her to have the painting as a parting gesture when he told her that he was entering into a 'proper marriage.' His parents would never have her, seeing as she was just a laundress at the time—she married a man who made a fortune later—and Terrence was an affluent artist from a respected family. So she left with only *Dream Rising* and her pride."

As they locked gazes, there was none of the vitriol that the previous generations of their families had woven into the fabric of this story.

There'd never been any of that between them.

No, there were just the misty memories of sensually wrapped arms and legs that had shaped Juliana's perception of what love and passion should be.

It should burn into you, she thought. *Through you. It should control your every move and breath as you merged and became one out of two.*

For a moment, it seemed as if tendrils from the past were drawing her and Tristan together.

Closer...

Closer.

She felt his hand near her thigh, but this time, she inched her leg nearer to him, inviting.

A server appeared again, delivering their food.

Restaurant, she reminded herself.

They were in public, not alone.

Not yet...

Jiro readied his chopsticks and picked up his bowl; it was acceptable to use the sticks to slurp the ramen straight into your mouth here.

But before he did, he said, "That's an intriguing tale."

Juliana idly stirred her broth, which held the noodles, tofu and an assortment of vegetables. She wasn't hungry for food—not with her stomach so upside-down and around.

Not with Tristan sitting so nearby.

He hadn't made a move to eat, either, and she wondered if he was feeling the same way, if he was thinking about what would happen once they left the restaurant.

Jiro swallowed his food, then said, "Forgive me, but I must tell you about a slight complication in these negotiations that will be solved quite easily, if I may. I discovered only a half hour ago that *Dream Rising* didn't arrive in its expected shipment."

Juliana stopped stirring her ramen. If she'd wondered whether they were being set up for competitive tension before, she was certain of it now. Maybe the painting really had been misdirected, but the dealer was milking it for all it was worth.

Tristan laughed, just as if he were thinking the same thing, and the rumble of the sound abraded her, especially since she knew what that laugh felt like chest-to-chest with him, skin-to-skin.

Jiro was laughing, too, as he put his bowl on the table. "I expect the painting presently. It was accidentally sent to an associate's gallery in New York since I often arrange showings there. My assistant is new, and he must have misunderstood my intentions. I'll redirect it here, but it's the dead of night in Manhattan, at the moment, so communication needs to wait until morning."

"And the price for the painting?" Tristan asked, picking up his chopsticks.

He didn't seem stressed about the news at all, even though she'd bet his family would freak out about the missing work, much as hers would.

Jiro was watching them both, as if sizing up their pocketbooks.

But then he smiled. "We can discuss price in a few days, when I have the painting in hand and you can look at the quality in person. I'll also have an authenticator present. And in light of this inconvenience, I'd like to invite both of you to my family's *ryokan* in Hakone when we're ready to do more business."

"A traditional Japanese hotel?" Tristan said. "That's good of you. I've thought about checking into one of those after I finished my business here. It would be convenient in Hakone because I was planning to visit one of my vintage-car associates who lives near Mount Fuji."

His leg fell toward hers, and she could feel it even though they weren't touching.

She'd read about the *ryokan* in her guidebooks. They could be little pieces of paradise, offering solitude and the romance of old Japan.

What might happen there? she wondered, picturing Tristan coming into her room, then closing the door behind him as her heartbeat throbbed and tangled.

"I appreciate the arrangements, too," she said to Jiro, while keeping her voice as level as possible.

Their host nodded just as "The Locomotion" dude from the counter wove past their table on his way to the back of the shop, gazing at Juliana and singing the cheery song again.

Entertained, Jiro turned around to speak to him.

Yes, she'd said to Tristan earlier.

And she showed him how much she meant it now, reaching over to rub her fingertips over his lower thigh, just above the knee.

He glanced at her, and she knew they had to get out of this restaurant as soon as they could.

As SASHA WANDERED through a diorama exhibit and then headed for the gift shop in Atami Castle, she glanced at her watch again, wondering when Juliana was going to call.

Anxiety raced through her, just as if she were at a starting line. She wanted her friend to put all this family business behind her and finally do something for herself for once. The way Sasha saw it, Juliana had caged herself by settling for Parisville after having been on her own, away from the Thomsens and their somewhat stifling affections.

That's why Sasha had left the place herself—because she wasn't much for small towns. She'd only landed there for a short time because of Chad, and maybe it'd been a good thing that they'd parted ways. She loved to travel, to be free to go where she wanted, even if she didn't always take full advantage of her liberty. Yet she had the option, and that's what counted. She could live as she wanted to without anyone to hold her back.

Sasha arrived in the gift shop, scanning the trinkets. She'd already decided not to think about Chad, although he'd come up in conversation earlier. Why ruin this trip by dwelling? She'd spent too long doing that already, and hanging around with Juliana and broadening their horizons was the best medicine, even if Sasha found the heat level of the research she had to do a bit daunting.

But she was here to knock the socks off her editor with this book, because she got the impression that her work could have enjoyed better sales in the past; she didn't know how many more chances she would have with this publishing house, and the future scared her.

Juliana's idea had captured what the public would want—exotic and erotic adventures for the single girl in Japan. And Sasha *would* make the most of it. She was going to attack this subject and increase her print runs so that her career would be assured for years to come.

When a petite salesclerk greeted her, then gestured over to a counter, Sasha smiled and got ready to dive into something other than the stateside travels she'd grown so used to.

Her destiny turned out to be a beach towel featuring what looked like a geisha in full costume.

The woman picked up a portable hairdryer and blew hot air over the towel, and the geisha's clothes disappeared, leaving the image buck-naked.

Unable to stop the laugh that overcame her, Sasha bowed, wished the clerk a good day and hightailed it out of the shop.

Okay, so the Japanese weren't quite as contained as she'd always thought. But kitschy souvenirs wouldn't make a bestselling book. She'd just have to look below the surface of their culture, the way that hot air had blown over the towel to reveal the erotic beneath its façade.

She fanned herself, then stopped. Hadn't Chad always told her she was too repressed? He'd always teased her about that—even made it a flirty challenge to try to loosen her up, but she never had.

Had that chased him away? What if she'd let her hair down and really given everything to him?

No use wondering, really. Not with Chad. But it made her think about any relationships she might have from now on, if the problems would still be the same.

As regret poked at her, she found her way to the basement of the castle, where a temporary art exhibit featured print copies that were lit from the back along the hallways.

Sensual prints.

Sasha looked around, finding no one else there.

Repressed? *Her?*

Suddenly, she didn't just need to write that book. She vowed to open her own to another chapter.

She sidled up to one of the pictures, her skin burning as she inspected another possible geisha, or probably a woman of pleasure, and a samurai warrior in flagrante delicto.

She swallowed, checking out the other prints, all with men who had long, thick penises and women whose private parts were bushier than a modern Western female kept her own pubic hair. The couples—sometimes more than just two—posed in various and interesting gymnastic positions.

Returning to the first piece, she pictured herself in the woman's place, then thought back to the last time she'd been to bed with a man.

Months ago. Not since Chad. Things had gotten busy with the career, and she'd gotten lazy.

Or maybe she just kept comparing everyone else to her ex.

When Sasha heard footsteps coming down the hall, she backed away from the print, trying to seem casually unaffected. But her skin was like blacktop in summer, heat wavering over it.

The footsteps stopped a ways back, and Sasha told herself not to look at the other viewer. It'd make her even more embarrassed to be here than she was now.

So much for becoming a wild woman, she thought.

Instead, she fidgeted with her high neckline, walking past print after print. But one of them made her pause a second too long: a picture of a man bent between a woman's legs. Yet that wasn't what caught the eye; it was that the lady was also reading a book, seemingly bored while the bemused male labored away.

Footsteps. Closer. Just one picture away.

Even closer now.

Then Sasha caught a whiff of sports soap. Detergent.

She closed her eyes as a world of memory took her over: nights on the couch going through magazines as she cuddled next to Chad, who would be reading *Fortune* or *Wired*. Sitting next to him in the car as he picked her up from the airport after a flight from her old home base in Reno, Nevada, and drove her to Parisville, where they were supposed to start building a life together.

She opened her eyes.

Chad?

Was he in Atami? Had his family tracked the painting here, too?

Then what was he doing in this castle?

She heard his voice behind her.

"Pity the guy." He was talking about the print. "Just look at him working so hard for the lady and she can't even put down her reading material."

Sasha rubbed her hands over her arms, hoping she could erase the chill bumps. "Maybe he should ask her what would please her. And if he listened, maybe he wouldn't need pity."

Silence bit between them while the night they'd broken up rushed back.

The night when Sasha had been called to attend a last-minute public relations opportunity—a book signing, three hours away, where she would join a few other more established writers from her freelance PR representative's list.

"You aren't seriously going to take off right now," he'd said after she'd ended the phone call.

But it was the *way* he'd said it that struck a deep, off-tune note in her—a disquiet that had gone untended ever since she'd come to Parisville for him. Ever since she'd made his life and his family a priority over everything else.

Maybe it was resentment that had broken them up, because she'd accused him of not believing that she'd ever amount to much. Accused him of being too stifling, also.

But he'd told her that she was the one who stifled herself, and she'd known that he was talking about her emotions, how she kept them close to her, how it was hard to give them all away.

Since then, she'd realized what had been repressing her: fear of losing herself and never getting it back once she got in too deep. She'd seen it happen to her mom, and even her brothers' wives, and she'd promised she'd never be them.

She'd kept that promise, even when it hurt.

And she'd left him.

Now, she faced Chad, hardly ready for the force of her reaction: a slam of desire and all the affection she'd thought had faded.

He hadn't changed an iota. Not one.

He still had the same wire-rimmed glasses that convinced her that he might just whip them off to go from this conservative masquerade to the sexy, lean lover beneath; the same button-down shirt hiding a physique that he honed through riding horses whenever he was at home; the same sparkling light-blue eyes that always told her so much about what he was feeling.

Well, maybe the eyes weren't sparkling so much right now.

"What're you doing here?" she asked, and the prideful sharpness of the question almost made her cringe.

He tucked his hands into his pockets. "I came over with Tristan for the painting, but it looks like Mr. Mori scheduled a dual appointment. Tristan's meeting with him and Juliana right now, and she told me you might be here—not that she was happy about letting me know, you understand. But I've been scouring the grounds to find you."

Sasha realized that her expression must've been giving away her agony at seeing him.

He searched her gaze. "I hope I didn't make a mistake in assuming it'd be okay to see you."

"No," she said. "We're both adults. We should be able to handle it."

They wordlessly started to walk away from the oral-sex print and to the next picture. She wished she could still read the more deeply buried signals that had developed between them long ago. Signals nurtured by two people who'd been on the cusp of truly committing.

At least, that's what she'd thought until they'd failed.

"There're a lot of things I've wanted to ask you," he said. "But I don't know where to start now."

She stopped walking, and he waited for her, his gaze caressing her until she had to look away.

"What sort of questions?" Again, with the pride. It'd been the only thing holding her together after the breakup. "How about this one—was I not exciting enough for you?"

"Sasha." In her peripheral vision, she saw him look at the ground. "Is that what it was all about?"

She sighed, tamping down her hurt. "No, you know there was a lot more."

"Yeah," he said. "And I know it wasn't right—me expecting you to drop everything and meld with my life without bringing much of yours into it. I didn't realize that until afterward, when I could think with more of a clear head."

Taken aback by his honesty, she wanted to come clean, too—to tell him that she'd had guilty moments afterward, as well. She'd wondered if she was selfish, especially since her mom seemed happy playing wifey to her dad's business. She smiled her way through a lot of cocktail parties, but Sasha didn't want to end up like that.

At her protective silence, he lowered the volume of the conversation, as if gentling something wild that might run away.

"Just tell me one thing," he said. "Are you happy now?"

Happy.

Was she?

As she searched for an answer, Chad took a step closer to her, then reached out to touch her cheek.

His fingertips brushed over her skin, and she sucked in a harsh breath at the anguish of what they'd lost.

They couldn't get back something that had already been broken. Besides, she wasn't even sure she could take the chance that they would fall into the same patterns that had scared her off the first time.

"I'm sorry," she said, grasping his hand in hers, waiting just one more second to remove it so she could feel him, remember him.

Then she backed away, turned around and continued down the hall.

Never looking back, even if she was dying to.

3

TRISTAN AND JULIANA left the ramen house, making their way down a hushed alley lined by store windows.

Her cheeks had an extra blush to them, even though a sulfur-laced sea breeze was now cooling the temperature. But there were still grates in the ground that seethed steam from mountain water sources that fed the hot springs.

The sight of her all flushed and bothered just made *him* hotter, encouraging him to picture her without clothing, bare and sweating in front of him.

Finally having her, Tristan thought. That's all he wanted. A chance to get what he hadn't before, then he'd be fine.

But how did a guy work up to that, even after the flirting touches, even after the sound of "yes" from Juliana's lips?

Something told him to handle her with care because he didn't want her to run off this time.

She stopped in front of a candy shop, smiling enough to show him that she wasn't just perusing the pastel, flowered goodies.

He lingered a foot away. "I don't know about you, but I'm only too glad that I won't have to get on the phone right away to call home with the news about the missing shipment."

"The time change gives us a reprieve, doesn't it? And so does this shipment error." She pushed the hair away from her neck, her skin soft and pink.

Damn, she'd taste good. All over.

She glanced at her bangle-type watch. "I suppose I should call Sasha and meet up with her now."

He knew she was testing him, seeing if he'd meant what he'd said back at the restaurant.

"Don't," he whispered.

She lowered her hand, gave him a look that wrapped his belly inside out.

"I'm staying in Tokyo," he said. "Are you in Atami?"

"No, I'm in the big city, too, since Jiro's gallery is there. Sasha and I are in the Shinjuku District near the train station."

When she told him exactly where they'd booked a room, he smiled at how close they actually were.

"We're practically neighbors," he said. "Just like in Parisville."

"Not the same."

"No," he said. "Not nearly the same."

She shot him a glance that could've meant a lot of things, but he hoped it offered a subtle invitation.

To do what? He wasn't quite sure yet, but he was set on discovering the possibilities while they could get away with it, so far from their real lives.

Until Jiro Mori had information about the painting's location, time was all theirs.

Could he have her in his hotel room within the next couple of hours?

Clearly, it was taking him too long to decide just how to go about getting her there gracefully, because he could see Juliana adopt a look of uncertainty as she wandered away from the candy-store window.

"I imagine you've got a lot of plans for this trip," she said. "When you get back to the city, I mean."

Still testing him.

He followed, off to pursue her in this lazy chase.

But he liked this—how they were circling each other, getting closer, semi-acknowledging that no one knew who they were and wouldn't care about their pasts or histories. Not here, not now.

"I'm a fly-by-the-seat-of-my-pants kind of guy," he said, "so I don't have any set plans."

They came to a dark, recessed entryway that was partially blocked by a vertical half door.

She glanced at it with those vivid eyes that were twinkling with what he thought might be mischief. She had looked the same way that first night, after he'd kissed her and she'd grabbed his T-shirt to draw him against her so she could kiss him right back.

Now, she backed into the alcove.

His body didn't wait for his brain to form another thought—not that he would've listened to any she's-just-gonna-leave-you-again warnings, anyway.

He followed her until the half door and the dimness hid them both.

"What's this?" he asked.

She smiled as she leaned back against a wall and tilted her head, as if running through those same warnings he'd rashly disregarded.

Then something in her eyes shifted, and he knew he had her.

"Back in the ramen house," she said, "it seemed as if we'd come to an agreement."

"About what?"

He wanted to hear her say it—that he'd always been her secret desire. His heart was shredding his chest, making so much noise that he could've sworn his pulse was audible.

"About…" she swallowed "…forgetting everything else and seeing what might've happened with us. Just this once."

He gently took her by the silk of her shirt near the waist. In the hushed light, she slid a low glance to his hand.

"I didn't want to say this out there," she said.

"Where people might see and hear?"

"I do keep promising myself that I won't cause any international incidents, Tristan. Public displays of affection aren't the norm here."

Her uplifted gaze dared him to do more, so he tightened his grip on her shirt, pulling her closer, breaths away.

Then a whisper.

God, her scent…

He became aware of people shuffling by outside the half door, and he let go of her shirt. Even so, his body stayed on red alert, his blood pumping.

"You know what a love hotel is, Juliana?" he asked, liking how her name sounded. He realized that he'd only said it out loud during the rare moments when it'd been necessary. That he'd mainly kept it inside.

At the mention of the hotel, her gaze got all the brighter. "It's a Japanese institution, a so-called fashion hotel where people can rent rooms for short times for 'rest.' For assignations, really."

"You did your homework." He tugged at her shirt. "The rooms can have different themes. Anything that gets a couple going. And they're very private."

"Good for keeping secrets."

He wound the material of her shirt around his fingers, bringing her near again, until their lips were inches apart.

"Maybe we can find a room that resembles that back-seat," he said.

When she laughed, her breath skimmed his mouth. "Or maybe something a little more comfortable."

He planted his other hand against the wall, just over her shoulder, loving how her mouth moved around every word.

What else could her lips do?

"By the time we take a train back to Tokyo," he whispered, his voice graveled, "it'll be late afternoon. We could meet, walk to the Kabuki-cho section—the red-light district—and find us a cultural experience."

Her breathing seemed shaky. "I heard that those hotels cater to Japanese people only. I don't know how true that is, but we don't even speak the language."

"I might be able to get by." At her curious glance, he added, "Lots of self-education."

He hadn't been kidding, but it'd sounded like a double entendre, and that seemed to amuse her.

"And what would I tell Sasha?" she whispered.

"Everything. Nothing." He lowered his mouth closer to hers until they were all but touching. "Anything."

They breathed against each other, each passing second increasing the pressure in his head, his groin.

But then she spoke.

"One condition."

His cock was pounding by now, so he would agree to rope the moon if that's what she wanted. "Name it."

She drew back from him a bit, not even an inch, but enough to send a dagger to his belly.

"When we get back home," she said, "it'll be like nothing ever happened here. I don't want to cause any more tension than already exists."

For an instant, he wondered if, all these years, he'd kept his affair with Juliana quiet for nothing. He'd been too young to know as much as he did now about the history of Terrence and Emelie.

Would everyone actually applaud Tristan if they learned that he'd nailed a Thomsen—just as Terrence had once so thoroughly seduced Emelie before things had gone to hell between them?

If Tristan were to walk in his great-great-grandfather's footsteps, would that prove the Coles were the masters of the situation? That the Thomsens were submissive?

He held back a frown. Sometimes it seemed that Gramps purposely ignored how much Terrence had loved the angry Emelie. Based on family lore, Terrence had possessed such feeling for her that no other woman had ever captured his heart again—not even his wife.

Yet Emelie had gotten her revenge by taking that painting.

At least, that's what the family said.

But the feud didn't matter right now. Not with the

heady scent of Juliana's hair winding through him like a corkscrew to his gut. Not with her so close, so warm, so much the fantasy that had the chance to come to fruition.

"Mum's the word," he said. "I won't tell a soul."

She exhaled, warm and moist against his lips. Tristan got closer, just a moan away from her mouth.

But then someone called out in what sounded like Aussie-accented English from outside, and she straightened, as if realizing where they were.

Before he could even open his mouth, she'd untangled herself from him and slipped away, out of their hiding place.

He moved out of the alcove, too, finding her standing in the alley, sunlight bringing out the silver of her long hair. He wondered if she was still just as blond between her legs.

The mere thought brought a tug to his cock.

"Let's meet up at your hotel. I'll call you in a few hours to tell you I'm waiting in your lobby," he said. "Be ready, Juliana."

She smiled, turned, and said over her shoulder while moving away, "I've been ready for longer than you can imagine."

Then she flashed him a smile and was gone, just as quickly as she'd appeared only two hours before.

WHEN JULIANA MET UP with Sasha at the Adult Museum, she didn't say a word to her friend about Tristan and the love-hotel date, even though she was as jumpy and excited as the little animated bunny that had marked her cab's progress on the GPS screen.

Truthfully, after Juliana had apologized for not being able to call to warn Sasha, she'd been expecting her friend to tell *her* all about Chad showing up at the castle so unexpectedly. But when her friend didn't initiate any discussion about it other than acknowledging that he'd come and gone, Juliana let the subject lie, knowing when to leave her alone.

Sasha internalized a lot, and she would no doubt share the details later, when she was ready.

But it wasn't as if Juliana was talking, either. Even after they saw things like whale genitalia and mermaid breasts at the Adult Museum, visited the hot springs, then returned to Tokyo, Juliana kept the most private events of the afternoon to herself.

She would tell Sasha everything else later, too, she thought. And it wasn't because Sasha would disapprove. No way. Juliana just didn't want anything—not even a surprised look from her friend—to remind her that she was going against her family's wishes.

Nothing was going to stop her from this one-time assignation. She was going to fulfill the biggest fantasy ever, going to pursue what she wanted, no matter what anyone else's opinion might be.

For now, at least.

At her hotel, which offered pretty much the same comforts you'd expect in the West, Juliana showered, then donned an outfit she'd intended to wear when she and Sasha went out at night: knee-high black boots, a short checkered skirt and a white blouse that modestly tied at the waist.

She wanted Tristan to see that she'd dressed for him,

wanted to feel sexier than she had in the conservative skirt she'd been sporting earlier.

She wanted to get it *all* back: the rush of a youthful, taboo encounter, the hopeful euphoria of getting away with it.

Nonchalantly, she waited by the phone for Tristan's call while studying her phrase book. Sasha was doing online research about Atami; she was even talking about returning to the resort town for a more extensive look into the spas since their visit had been cut short today—Sasha had said she was worn out, much to Juliana's relief.

"You sure it's okay that I'm staying in here and not checking out the department stores with you?" Sasha asked, turning away from her laptop, which was perched on a desk.

"Not at all." Guilt tapped at Juliana because she'd told Sasha a tiny white lie about going to the stores surrounding nearby Shinjuku Station. "You've got work to do, and I'm all for striking out on my own until tonight."

"Okay then. Give me four hours to be ready for dinner and whatever else the night might hold?"

"Gotcha. I'm just going to catch up on useful shopping phrases first, then I'm out of here."

Juliana went back to her guidebook while Sasha faced her computer. Within the next fifteen minutes, the phone on the nightstand rang.

Affecting a now-whoever-could-be-calling-us? face, Juliana answered.

Tristan's deep voice sounded on the other end. "Hi."

"Hi" could have meant something other than a greeting the way he'd said it. He made the word into a promise.

"You ready?" he asked.

"Yes." Then just to fool Sasha that much more, she added, "Um, I'm sorry, I don't speak Japanese."

She hung up the phone and shrugged at her friend, who was watching with interest.

"Wrong number." Juliana rose from the bed and stretched, then stowed her little guidebook in her purse. "I'm off and running now."

"Have fun. Be careful out there."

"Me?" She grinned and moved toward the door. "I'm as careful as they come."

Sasha smiled and waved goodbye, and Juliana felt like a turd.

But she'd tell her friend all about Tristan and the love hotel when she got back. Heck, she was betting she wouldn't be able to keep her mouth shut after the time she'd have with him, and if there was one person she could trust to keep things quiet, it was her pal.

She took the elevator to the lobby, then glanced around to find Tristan leaning against a wall near the front desk.

Her heart—and just about everything else—gave a jump at the sight of him.

He'd obviously showered off the humidity, too, because in addition to a change of clothes—he was wearing a dark button-down shirt with dark jeans—his devil-may-care hair was wet and combed away from his face. The style only served to make the angles of his cheekbones more lethal, the gray of his eyes more knee-buckling.

Lordy.

As she walked over to him, he straightened, his eyes darkening to a shade that almost scared her, it was so intense.

The bad boy, she thought. Hers for a few wonderful hours.

"Hey." She realized she was clutching her purse, so she relaxed.

"Hey. You look…"

His tongue seemed to be tied.

"Non-rumpled?" she asked with a laugh. "I thought I should change clothes."

"I was going to say you look good. But you know what I mean by good, right?"

"I suppose so."

He shook his head, chuckled, and her heart melted a bit, because he seemed sort of adorable, as though they really were in high school and he'd come to the door to take her on their first date, which would be out there for everyone to see in a perfect world.

But she could guarantee that this "date" would involve more than an innocent movie or Red Lobster dinner.

They started to walk out of the lobby, and when they came to the doors, he held one open for her.

A right-raised gentleman, she thought, wondering how many sides there were to this quiet, mysterious man she'd barely gotten to know, even when they'd been so intimate with their bodies.

He must have changed over the years, and she found herself wondering how.

Outside, the air was still thick, but with the added smell of the city stitched into it. While they headed for the red-light district, she caught him giving the eye to her short skirt.

"What, do you have a schoolgirl complex?" she asked.

"I wouldn't say that as much as your skirt shows your legs off real well. There isn't a man alive who wouldn't appreciate that."

His compliment sounded so sincere that she wasn't sure how to respond, so she just said, "Thank you," and kept walking.

Soon, they passed the department stores where she was supposed to be shopping and, after having to look at a map only once, they found the Kabuki-cho, where the late-afternoon sun bathed neon-flared pachinko parlors, restaurants and bars. The streets seemed to be lined with signage, character-filled squares piled upon each other like techno building blocks. Japan was so full of silent mysteries, loaded significance behind each gesture. Even the graceful curves of the alphabet seemed like stories left untold to her eyes.

Here it began, she thought. Where she started to explore.

Who knew what would be hiding behind all those closed doors?

They came upon a place with a blue light shining over its walls.

"This is one of them?" she asked. "I thought the façade would be a little crazier."

"Outside the city, there're love hotels shaped like UFOs and ships—anything to draw attention."

"How about…inside?"

He gave her a knowing glance. "I guess there's been some 'public morals' overhaul, and a lot of hotels had to tone it down. But this is a red-light district, and it should be just the escape we're looking for. I chose this one off the Internet, just to be sure."

They found a discreet entrance, and he opened the door for her, but she hesitated.

Now that they were down to it, she was almost afraid to go inside. What if sex with Tristan turned out to be a disaster? What if reality took away every dream that'd gotten her through all the disappointing dates of the past few years?

But when Tristan held out his hand, that was all it took.

With a held breath, she accepted the invitation, letting him lead her over the threshold into an otherwise empty lobby dominated by an automated payment system and a large board featuring lit pictures of the available rooms.

Her choice of fantasies, she thought. But, really, any room would do as long as Tristan was in it, in the flesh.

She barely saw the options: an S&M-themed dungeon-looking thing. A disco palace. A Hello Kitty haven.

Nothing with a car however.

Then she saw the room with a pool and waterfall, and she knew it was the one.

Tristan, all wet. All hers.

Without any discussion, he pushed the button, which resulted in the appearance of a key card and a light that switched on over a door to the side.

Looked like they wouldn't have to speak Japanese after all.

They went through the door, down the hall, until they came to another room with a light on to indicate this was theirs.

With a confident grin, Tristan opened it, ushering her in first as her heart stamped in an uneven rhythm.

This is it, she thought as she heard the tumble of a waterfall beckoning from behind a wall that blocked their view of it. The place smelled of cleaning products and a subtle jasmine scent. *This is your chance to let nothing else but water come between you and him.*

They passed the large, shining bathroom, which looked to be stocked with a bounty of toiletries, then rounded the wall to find a modest lagoon-shaped rock pool to the right, with the small waterfall flowing into it. It dominated everything, including the velvet-roped swing that waited over the shallow end. Even the opposite side of the room seemed dwarfed by comparison, although that was the part that held a king-size bed decorated with exotic leaf patterns and condoms on the pillows. Next to it sat a big-screen TV with a DVD collection, a karaoke system and a video-game console.

Juliana glanced at the pool again, her clit already hardening, her breasts already beading.

From behind, Tristan slid his arms around her, his hands gliding over her waist, then her belly.

Bang—her body remembered everything: the turn-on of sneaking around, the wiggling excitement of his fingers exploring places that no one had ever touched before.

He was still the only one who made her anticipate it so much.

She pushed back against his growing erection, feeling the ridge of it, remembering how it'd felt under her shy hands way back when.

And how it was going to feel now.

"We're finally here," he whispered in to her ear. "And you're all mine tonight, Juliana Thomsen."

4

TRISTAN WAS DOING everything within his power to keep from tearing off her clothes and slipping into her.

He was hard and ready, had been that way ever since this afternoon when she'd pulled him into that alcove.

But when he'd seen her in that short skirt and those boots?

Harder and readier.

"What's your pleasure first?" he asked, gliding his hands from her belly to her ribs. "We're in here for three hours, Juliana. We've got time to do whatever you want."

When he nuzzled her just below the ear, she gasped, and the sound was like a physical thrust, escalating his need for her.

But she made no move to look around, instead staying just where he wanted her to be—in his arms, softer and more pliant by the second.

He kissed her neck, paused to allow the past to catch up with the present, then kissed her between the jaw and ear where she was as warm and fragrant as a hothouse flower. She'd been sensitive there back then, and she sure was now as she leaned her head back against him, arching her neck.

"Damn, you taste good," he said. "I remember that."

"I'm sure remembering a lot, too," she said, her voice strained.

Was she?

Something in his chest flared at the possibility that he'd remained with her just as constantly as she'd stayed with him.

But that wasn't the point of this.

Sex, he thought. *A man taking what should've been his long ago.*

He smoothed his thumbs to just below the curves of her breasts while gently biting her ear.

She moaned in bliss.

There. But that was only going to be the beginning of the sounds, the cries, the screams for more that he'd longed to hear….

Turning her head to the side, she nestled against his throat, rubbing her cheek against him. Her hair rained against his skin, undoing him because the sensation had been so forbidden until now, and reminding him of how he'd felt when she'd left town and him.

Empty, he thought.

But now, as he eased his palms upward to cup her breasts, he filled himself.

She sucked in a breath, rocking back against him, her ass soft against his erection. He circled his thumbs over her nipples, vaguely thinking that her breasts had always been small, firm, perfect.

It was as if she was meant for him, but he knew better than to think that way. This was only a bubble in time, one night when they could pretend that there was nothing else out there to return to.

As he pressed one palm downward, she raised her arms and locked her hands behind his neck, giving her leverage to arch away from him again, straining, sexy.

He reached underneath that short, checkered skirt, coaxing his fingers between her legs, where she was already slick against her lace panties.

Her readiness thrilled him, stirring him into a light-headed mess of diminishing control.

He bent, slid his arm under her knees, picked her up and headed toward the pool where that waterfall was banging away as powerfully as lust was demolishing him.

She gaped at him, her lips parted, her eyes wide, her face flushed.

"What're you doing?" she asked.

"Getting you even wetter."

His direct way of answering seemed to deepen the color on her cheeks. He hadn't been that way when he was a teenager—he'd been more reticent, not going for what he wanted.

He brought her to the edge of the water.

"Wait," she said. "Boots. I need to take off my boots."

He set her on her feet, cursing the interruption. He was ready for her *now.*

As she unzipped the sides of her footwear, the sound gnawed into him, running over his skin like the nails she'd whisked over his bare back one night when they had kissed until they'd both been out of breath.

Feeling the same giddiness now—like a young guy with his whole life ahead of him—he doffed his own shoes, socks, shirt.

But when she backed into the pool with her skirt and

top still on, he paused in the rest of his strip-off. She was taking in his bare chest, and the haziness of her gaze told him that she liked what she saw.

"You've filled out," she said. "Not that you were skinny back then, but…"

"Are you going to get back here, or do I need to come after you?" Gruff, needful. He couldn't hide it.

She pushed back her hair from her face, slicking it with water as she watched him, as if not knowing for sure *what* she wanted him to do, and he noticed there was a slight tremble to her hands.

It hit him: they weren't dabbling in tentative backseat experimentation anymore. He knew it, she knew it.

There was so much more at stake now. And afterward they would have to go back to Parisville, resume life, go on with…

He didn't want to think about being alone in his cabin, looking out the window in the direction of the Thomsens' property.

In the water, Juliana reached behind her for the velvet-chained swing. When she found it, she held on to the flat, vinyl-cushioned seat, as if seeking the balance they'd both lost upon just entering this room.

The water came to her upper thighs in this shallow portion; he could see it got deeper near the waterfall. The fringe of her skirt skimmed the surface, and he wished it were his hands, his mouth drenching her instead of the pool's water.

Unwilling to wait for the time it'd take to shuck off his jeans, he entered the pool.

She took in a breath, but unstoppable now, he dragged

through the water until he came to a stop right in front of her, so near that she had to tilt her chin up to look him in the eye.

Without a word, he lifted her skirt, and she held tighter to the swing.

"I used to love how you felt down here," he said, easing a finger between her legs, stroking upward and making her wince. "I used to love how you sounded when I touched you like this."

"Tristan…"

Hearing his name from her drove him harder, and he reached both hands under her skirt, catching the sides of her panties, pulling them down.

One leg up, sliding those undies down and off, then the other.

In the end, he held the scant material.

White lace, he thought before tossing them to the pool's edge. Back in the day, she'd worn undies with hearts.

He liked the lace better.

She was already holding on to the velvet-covered chains of the swing, anticipating his next move, when he lifted her into the seat.

All the while, they never looked away from each other, almost as if the warm water around them was all a dream that they'd snap out of if they surrendered eye contact.

He raised her skirt just the slightest to catch a peek beneath.

Still blond.

Throat choked, he snagged her gaze again, and tension thundered around them, as palpable as the beating of the waterfall.

He spread her thighs, her skirt riding up to reveal more light hair surrounding the pink of her, and adrenaline swallowed him, his mind spinning.

He'd gotten inebriated on her kisses before, but he hadn't put his mouth on her most sensitive part. And he wanted to, wanted it badly right now.

Then he would have the rest of her.

Then he would be satisfied.

He pulled on the swing's seat, bringing her toward him, wrapping his arms under her legs so that her calves hooked over him. She leaned to one side of the swing, holding on to the chain, her lips moist and parted as she watched.

He watched back for a moment.

Beautiful Juliana Thomsen. Not a dream, not a figment of his idle musings.

And not the good girl he'd always imagined. Not anymore.

As if to urge him on, she used one hand to pull her skirt back.

Like a starved man, he scooped the swing closer and pressed his mouth to the warm plumpness of her.

Yes, he thought, losing his mind altogether. *Juliana.*

He licked, making her wetter, and she groaned, pushing her hips forward.

"Just like that," she said. "Oh, just like that."

He went at her harder, nuzzling against her, using his tongue to taste every inch, then to enter her just as he'd imagined doing with his cock back then. He would've loved her a long time if he'd only gotten the opportunity….

Something gave him pause.

Love.

Loved her *how?*

The thought shocked him, and it only grew stronger as she buried her fingers in his hair, pulling at him, encouraging him with soft mewls and moans.

Wanting to give her more, he brought one of his thumbs to work her clit, pressing, circling around and around until she was grinding against him.

"Tristan," she said. "Keep going…"

It became his mission to get it done, to make her sob, to send her falling into him and to have her ask for more.

So he laved her until she was so far forward on the swing that she lost equilibrium and tumbled out of it, sending them both into the water.

He pulled her to a stand, and she pushed her wet hair away from her face, panting.

But she wasted no time, grabbing him, pulling him down for a searing kiss, her wet shirt plastered against his chest.

His head swam at the touch of her lips and, for a desperate moment, he slowed down, stroking his hands under her jaw to hold her.

There. She was his, and he wanted to relish it, just as he'd done so long ago.

She responded, opening wider for a kiss that seemed to last forever as they tested, explored, falling farther and farther into each other, into a hole that seemed to expand underneath him.

He lost himself in thoughts of sweet blond hair, smooth skin, violet eyes that pierced like the edges of a disappearing rainbow.

He was falling, not necessarily downward, just…

Away.

Away from the reason he'd come to Japan.

Away from everything he'd promised to the others at home.

JULIANA WAS ABOUT TO BURST, her body pounding, her lungs so shallow she could barely breathe.

Even the hint of stubble on his chin sparked her closer and closer toward a climax, burning her skin, lighting a fire deep in her belly, then higher.

Higher.

But something within her was trying to push that orgasm down, fighting it.

Was it because she didn't want her first time with Tristan to end so quickly?

Or was it because…?

No, she wouldn't think of guilt or betrayal—concepts that only seemed to apply to the world outside this room.

She *wouldn't* think about any of it now.

As she kissed and kissed him, she ran her hands over his muscled back, the water making her urgent caresses slippery.

Touching him felt like coming home for some reason. It felt…right, just as it had years ago.

So why hadn't she gone out on a limb to be with him?

Why hadn't she been strong enough back then?

She beat away the thought that she wasn't strong enough even now, after so much time had passed; all she and Tristan wanted was to scratch an itch, to give in to temptation this once.

It's only sex now, she thought. They were grown-up enough to handle an affair then forget about it.

He started to lead her toward the edge of the water, to a selection of pool toys neatly stacked on fake rock shelves.

"You're so close," Tristan said, his voice rumbling through his chest, vibrating into her. "How close?"

As he effortlessly sat her on the lip of the pool, she whispered into his ear, "Very. Just keep on doing what you're doing."

He took her face between his hands, and her sex ached. So did her heart.

No, she thought. Not her heart. It didn't belong anywhere near this, even though it kept reminding her that it was about to explode.

As Tristan scanned the toys, which included such whimsical choices as water wings, plastic tennis rackets and squirt guns, he smiled that bad-boy smile she'd always adored. His long hair flopped over his brow, giving him a dark charm.

"I want this to last a long time, Juliana." He inspected a small inflatable manga dog, then moved on. "A long time."

She moved her hips, hurting for him.

"Patience," he said. "We've waited years for this. It'll be worth it."

A thrill spun through her.

Water gleamed over his skin, his streamlined muscles, turning her on all over again, her heartbeat flailing and wheeling.

He took hold of her shirt, which stuck to her like a

second skin. Her nipples crested against it, hardly hiding how much she craved him.

He deftly began to undo her top button. Then the next one. The next.

All the while, her chest rose and fell, spiked by her pulse.

After removing her shirt, he did the same to her bra, discarding both. But before he got to her skirt, he paused to run his knuckles over one naked breast, as if to memorize every sensitized part, giving him fuel for when they'd walk out of this hotel and go their separate ways.

He brought her nipple to an even more agonizing peak.

"After you left," he said, "I'd dream about you every night, remembering how you looked. Your skin. Your tiny waist. How your chest rose and fell with every breath. How you looked at me like you're looking at me now."

No one had ever sounded so romantic to her—or, at least, they hadn't come off as genuine. His words yanked at something that felt like strings around her heart, jerking it into an even sharper rhythm than before.

She didn't know what to say, but when he leaned over to kiss her other breast, she didn't have the oxygen to spare, anyway.

Her head dipped back as she bucked, and he caught her legs on either side of him.

"Now," he said. "As much as I like this skirt, it needs to go."

No arguments.

She reached behind to unzip it, and when she'd fumbled her way through that, she pushed the material down.

He helped her, then tossed the material to the side, leaving her vulnerable to him, the air tickling her clit.

He took up a squirt gun, then used his fingers to open her.

Then he shot a line of warm water at her.

She gasped as it hit her, shocking her through and through.

He brought it closer, this time bathing her clit in a steady stream of pressure.

It was at that point that she pretty much fell to pieces, her arms losing strength as she slumped to the ground, her limbs disintegrating even as she went tighter...skin puckering, core retracting, sharpening...

Meanwhile, Tristan used his other hand to massage her belly, and she lifted her arms above her head, just like the mist in the painting they both wanted.

Reaching, needing....

Almost there. Oh, so close—

He pulled her back into the pool, and she was so dizzy that she hadn't even noticed him shedding the rest of his clothing; she only realized it when she felt his bare arousal against her leg.

"Condom," he said, dragging her to the shallow side of the pool, where he'd have to get out to grab one from the nearby bed.

"Wait," she said on a croak of breath. "I'm clean."

"Me, too."

"And I'm on the pill."

Maybe she wasn't thinking straight, but all she wanted was him—the unsheathed feel of him inside of her. It would make this different from the other men she'd been with. She trusted him, too, because he'd kept their summer fling a secret when she'd asked him to, when he'd had the chance to brag about it.

He'd respected her and his family too much to do that, and that spoke volumes about Tristan.

He gazed at her for a moment, those light-gray eyes drawing her in and making her feel as if she was floating.

But, then again, she literally was, as he switched direction in the pool, away from where he'd been going toward the shallows, and guided her to deeper water, up to his chest, near the waterfall where both their bodies took on buoyancy.

His tone was strained. "Juliana…"

There it was again—that sincerity of feeling, the assurance that he needed her as badly as she needed him.

She wrapped her legs around him as his feet stayed anchored to the bottom of the pool. The waterfall sprayed them, poking at her skin like tiny needles.

In his eyes, she saw so much: tenderness, profound desire, the excitement of finally getting what he wanted.

He grabbed her by the hips, and she prepared herself, taking in a deep breath…

…then heaving it out when he slid into her.

For a moment, she didn't move.

It was just as she'd known it would be. He filled her up, hard and thick, and she'd never felt so whole.

This was what she'd been holding out for. Tristan. Two becoming one, misting, melting…

Slowly, sinuously, she moved her hips, grinding, taking him deeper. Taking as much as she could get of him.

"Juliana," he said again, and the naked passion in his

tone aroused her that much more, pushing up a foreign pressure, through her belly, her stomach, a knife point of possibility.

She labored, churned, the water waving around them.

He dug one hand into her hair, grasping it, forcing her to look down at him as they moved together, searching for that next level, that final barrier.

His eyes were so beautiful, she thought. Gray, light and clear...

But, in the back of her mind, something was still holding her back.

A climax was just heartbeats away, as an inner pressure moved to her chest, around her heart....

Almost there...

Almost—

He came first, exploding into her, just about ripping her apart and making her expand until she almost broke.

But she didn't.

Dammit, why not? Why couldn't she...?

He reached down and helped her along, strumming her.

She embraced him, bringing him against her, pressing her face against his head as she worked her hips.

She remembered that last night, when she hadn't wanted to leave him, when she'd thought her heart was getting chiseled out of her chest....

Then finally, *finally*—

She cried out as an orgasm slammed her, depriving her of a heartbeat and breath, suspending everything in a void in time.

When she came back to herself, she had no idea how long she'd blanked out.

Trembling, slumping against him, she slid down his body until they came face-to-face, panting against each other.

They stayed there for what seemed like an hour, holding each other, not letting go, and then with every passing second, reality nudged her, growing, taking over.

Her family.

What would happen if they found out?

Pressured by the disappointment she knew they'd feel, she kissed Tristan one more time, then pushed away, heading for the side of the pool.

As she reached the edge, she looked back to find him running a hand through his hair, questions clearly written on his sculpted face.

Well, she had questions, too, and unfortunately, her conscience was giving her answers she didn't want to hear.

5

IN HIS WEAK-LIMBED AFTERMATH, Tristan lazily dipped under the water, then moved through the pool on his way to the waterfall.

She'd been everything he'd been hoping for—more than any other woman in this world. More than any dream he'd ever satiated himself with at night, when he'd pictured her under him, on top of him in all those scenarios he'd created in his fevered mind.

So what was with the space Juliana had put between them now?

Actually, he didn't even have to ask because he knew.

The painting. The negotiations that only signified something much larger between them.

But why had all that crap entered into something that was supposed to be an escape?

He maneuvered under the waterfall, allowing the liquid to patter down on him, cooling his body. At the same time, he watched her at the side of the pool where she was recovering, too.

The moments passed, his body mellowing while the water lapped at her waist as she kept her back to him.

Her slim, toned, tempting back.

"Not bad for a Thomsen," he finally called over to her once he'd fully gathered himself.

She glanced over her shoulder with a look that pounded him just as surely as the water.

"Not bad for a Cole," she answered.

She smiled, just as if they were back to seducing each other, then turned all the way toward him. Water glistened over her small breasts, the pale-pink pebbled tips. Her stomach was flat, and he thought about how her whole body had curved like willow branches under his hands.

When she moved through the pool in his direction, it was suddenly harder to take in air.

"Your family," she said. "What would they say if they knew you'd brought me to a tawdry love hotel of all places?"

A cutting laugh escaped him. "Why're you worrying about what they or anyone else would say or do? We don't have to be thinking about that. Not right now."

She paused, floating in the water a few feet away, where the waterfall sent stray splashes over her. Her gaze became distant as she smiled again, more to herself than anything.

"Yeah," she said. "You're right. I can't have their opinions controlling my every move. I keep telling myself that, but hearing you say it drives the notion home."

Tristan tried not to let her see how much that pleased him. He was no advice-giver, but she made it sound as if he were good at it.

"No one," he said, his body ticking—a time bomb set to go off inside her again—"is going to know what happened here in Japan. Not even Chad. I can keep my mouth shut."

Even though it was a promise he would keep, there was

a part of him that wanted to shout out that she'd been with him.

Juliana Thomsen, who'd been the one to leave him when he would have sucked up his courage and defied his family for her, if she'd only asked him to.

Being with her made it easy to admit it now.

She pushed through the pool until she came all the way to him, the waterline coming to her neck as she held up her hand, her pinkie extended.

"What's this?" he asked.

"Pinkie promise."

"What the hell's a pinkie promise?"

"A binding vow. Like blood brothers." She laughed, and the sound almost took him under. "Didn't you ever hear of this?"

"I guess. Tom Sawyer and Huckleberry Finn were blood brothers."

"Then we can be blood..." She searched for a description.

He helped her out. "We can just call it our little secret."

Giving in to her—hell, it was way too easy—Tristan held out his pinkie.

Her eyes went bright as he hooked onto her.

The sound and vibration of the waterfall suspended, leaving a vacuum around them, and there was just her.

Juliana.

As their fingers tightened, he realized that he'd never felt this kind of connection. He'd never even gone beyond a few dates with a woman before one or the other of them lost interest.

Then again, he supposed he'd never really forgotten

Juliana. Maybe he'd even held out hope that he'd see her walking past the ranch some day. Right. Or more likely, during one of his infrequent trips to town, he'd see her in a diner or through the window of her family's bookstore, if he felt like causing some gossip by lingering too long in front of it.

He worked his pinkie out of hers, latching on to her hand instead and towing her closer to him.

Then he pulled her through the waterfall, bringing them both into a hollow, faux-rock minicave, where the rest of the room looked warped from behind the tumble of water.

The mist reminded him of the wan copy of *Dream Rising* his family displayed over his gramps's fireplace.

"So what do you think happened between Emelie and Terrence?" he asked. "I mean, what *really* happened?"

Juliana wrapped her arms around his shoulders. "I've always believed Emelie's letters. Then again, that's how I was raised, on her version of the story. But I chose to concentrate on the part where they were in love instead of everything that came afterward."

A romantic, he thought. He remembered how she'd loved to hear slow songs on the radio, and even in the short week they'd been together, he'd thought it said a lot about her, just like those books she'd read with women wearing silk dresses, leaning back in the arms of pirates.

"I've always thought Terrence's journals revealed everything," he said. His family had even sent along copies of the pages so Tristan could review them if needed on this trip.

He skimmed the wet hair away from her face, and her eyes went soft.

"Bottom line," he said gently, "is that there's got to be middle ground. Terrence and Emelie both saw the same situation in different ways. In reality, there's probably not a villain in their story."

"I just wish our indoctrinated elders felt the same way."

Tristan grinned. "They need to find hobbies, like we have. Some other kind of fulfillment."

They both laughed, and he deposited her into a rock nook.

"Fulfillment," Juliana repeated, leaning back, drawing her legs under her like a mermaid. "Now there's a concept that escapes me."

Although she was naked, laid out for the taking, he was more enthralled with what he saw in her bared gaze—an obvious hankering for something more than she'd found in life.

He knew what Juliana could've done with her talents. Top-notch grades, a bachelor's degree in Business Administration, a partner in a tour company she'd started in San Diego until she'd returned to Parisville... She could've gone places while he'd refrained from college and favored self-education.

But she'd ended up in the same situation he was in.

"I'm pretty sure," he said, "that we've both been swayed by what others have wanted our whole lives."

"Living up to expectations. Ain't it a bitch?"

He smiled, running his fingers over her toned calf. She had to be a jogger, he thought. Had to stay in shape somehow.

"Truthfully," he said, "I don't know what my gramps is expecting out of this."

"Same with my family. *Dream Rising* is gorgeous, and I really do understand the emotional attachment to it since it's part of our family history, but there's a..." She paused. "I suppose you'd say zealousness to have it that has nothing to do with its beauty."

"It's not about the art itself," he said.

"No. It's not. It's about domination to all of them."

He watched her, wondering what she personally saw in the picture. As far as he was concerned, the painted strokes were a flowing puzzle—something he almost had a grasp on but could never quite get.

She'd tilted her head, watching him, too, and the accessibility of her sympathetic gaze made him talk more.

"Before my dad passed on a few years ago, he told me that the family would expect me to feel the same way they do. But he told me to consider what was really going on before throwing myself wholeheartedly into the fray. When he was alive, he kept me away from it as much as he could."

"I was sorry to hear about your dad, Tristan," she said softly.

He knew she would've heard about how sudden and terrible his father's too-recent death had been, even from her family's place across town. A heart attack one night after dinner while Tristan had been working away in his garage.

"I appreciate your saying that," he said.

Behind him, the waterfall started to lose power, spilling to almost nothing but trickles, and Tristan realized that it must be on a timer.

"Sometimes I think that Gramps measures his life

against how he fares with your family," he continued. "He took the lead position in the feud back after the property-line dispute that you all won, and he hasn't let up since."

"My aunt Katrina's the same way. After she lost her husband, she started researching family trees and developing this uber-pride about our history. She's a nut about 'preserving' it, as she calls the campaign to get the painting."

Tristan rested his fingers on her knee, but he didn't let go. Her skin felt so smooth, comfortable against his own flesh.

"Yet here we are," he said, "representing their sides in these negotiations. You think we'll turn out like them?"

"Or," she said, almost sadly, "like Emelie and Terrence, hating each other afterward?"

A broken love affair, he thought. A sad waste of two people who could've had something if it wasn't for circumstance and maybe even pride.

He moved his hand from her knee upward, over the outside of her thigh, and she sighed, sinking down as she kept her eyes on him.

"Let's just think about the next two hours between *us,*" he said.

But even as he kissed her again, his mind was already racing ahead to tomorrow and how he could possibly stretch this one night of stolen bliss into two.

AFTER RETURNING TO THE hotel, Chad Cole had decided that the best way to pass the time would be to have a fine Japanese beer or two in the hotel's English-style pub.

As he relaxed in one of the deep, tastefully upholstered

chairs in the dim-lighting-and-etched-glass atmosphere, he tried not to think about this afternoon in the castle.

Tried not to think about how Sasha had walked away from him.

But what had he expected?

For months, he'd mentally flayed himself for what had happened between them, but every time he'd tried to pick up the phone to apologize, he would stop himself.

Wait a week, he would think. That way, Sasha wouldn't be as angry.

Instead, he had sent flowers at the five-month mark, and Sasha had thanked him with an e-mail—a clear sign that she wasn't open to any sort of personal contact.

Final is final, he'd thought, knowing Sasha didn't fool around when she made a decision.

In the heavy days afterward, Chad's family had revealed that they were relieved about the breakup. As intelligent and genial as Sasha was, they'd said, the family had never really taken to her. There was just something so…closed off.

Chad hadn't admitted to them that he'd thought so, too.

There were many other girls out there, they'd said— ones who were willing to leave their careers behind and were more open with their emotions.

Yet Chad had wanted to tell them—and convince himself—that just because Sasha was choosy with her words and gestures, that didn't mean she felt any less than the rest of them.

They didn't understand what he saw in her, but who could explain love? He couldn't elaborate on how the shy way she smiled made him feel protective and passionate at the same time. He couldn't diagram the pride he saw in her eyes when he told her about what he'd accomplished that day.

And he couldn't chat about the sex: how they fitted and moved together. How, every time, he'd believed that this would be the moment Sasha would finally let her hair down for good when they held each other, sweat-sticking body to body.

He'd told himself that one day she would expose the extent of her feelings, yet she never had, and he'd begun to wonder if he was only fooling himself, wonder if his love had only been one-sided and everyone but him had seen it. Yet that hadn't stopped him from going to her today in that castle, out of pure impetuousness.

Enough months had passed for her to reconsider, he'd thought, but he'd obviously been wrong....

By the time Tristan finally sauntered into the bar, Chad had plowed through five beers and, even then, the answers weren't any clearer. In fact, everything was a little murkier.

His cousin was tucking his rented international cell phone into his back jeans pocket. Chad vaguely noticed that he was wearing a different pair than earlier.

"Got the message you left under my door," Tristan said, taking a seat at the table. "How long have you been here?"

Chad realized that the other man's hair was wet, too. "An hour. Two. Hey, is it that humid out there? It looks like you jumped in a pool."

The shadow of a smile crossed Tristan's lips, and for some reason, Chad thought it resembled the type of grin a man wore when he was hiding a secret.

But his brain wasn't working well enough to pursue that idea. Sasha's face kept flashing over his mind's eye, blocking out everything else.

Tristan ran a hand through his hair. "I took a shower after I got back from wandering around outside."

"Long walk, pardner."

"Part of the time I was on the phone with Jiro Mori. He said the painting's being shipped from New York as we speak, and he expects it to be ready for us by the day after tomorrow."

"Honestly, I'm glad for this lag. I'm kind of enjoying myself here in the Land of the Rising Sun." Or maybe suns, since Chad was seeing double of just about everything at the moment.

"You're slurring," Tristan said.

Chad lifted up his half-full beer. "I certainly should be."

Tristan gave him a withering glance.

"Okay, okay," Chad said. "So seeing Sasha wasn't the best brainstorm I've ever had."

"Sasha." Tristan sank back in his chair, as if realizing it was going to be a long talk. "I should've guessed you got sloshed because of your ex."

"Not all of us were born with the Joe Cool gene."

At first, it looked as if Tristan were about to contradict him, but then his cousin's mouth set into a firm line.

Another weird vibe niggled at Chad, but it had nothing to do with Sasha, so he ignored it.

"She turned her back on me."

"You told me all about it earlier on the return trip."

"It's not right that she's in a hotel that's only a walk away and I'm here." Determination started burning in

Chad's belly, a screw-what-everyone-else-thinks blaze. "I'm not sure how to persuade her of it, but she's the one, Tristan. The only one."

His cousin paused before saying, "I hope you're not asking me for ideas about how to win her back or something, because I don't know squat about romance." He grinned. "Not really, anyway."

Then, after a second more of that strange grin, Tristan abruptly stood. "Let's go to the room, clean you up then get us some dinner."

"I'm having a constructive conversation here. Or I *was*."

Tristan finally turned back to his cousin, his brow furrowed. "You're serious about this."

"Couldn't be more."

Chad's chest felt as if it was being pulled apart, making the cliché about the broken heart seem painfully true. Seeing Sasha again had been like yanking open a stitched wound.

But he would've done it a second time, a third, just because he could've sworn that he'd seen something in her eyes—something hinting that she'd missed him as much as he'd missed her.

Tristan was gauging him, no doubt coming to the conclusion that Chad was one sorry idiot. But there was a flash of understanding, too.

Would his rogue cousin help him, out of the goodness of the heart Chad knew Tristan had somewhere beneath all the layers?

He thought he heard Tristan curse under his breath, not loudly enough to offend the servers or the few other customers. But definitely enough to reveal some reluctance.

"Come on then," his cousin said, extending a hand to help Chad to his feet. "There are those guidebooks in your room. Maybe we can look through them to find someplace romantic for this windmill-tilting of yours."

Chad put down his beer, ignoring Tristan's hand in favor of coming to a stand on his own.

"Thanks, pard," he said, patting his cousin on the shoulder. "You were always the only one who seemed to like Sasha."

They went up to his room, where Chad began to concoct a plan for winning over his true love once again.

AS SASHA STYLED HER HAIR into a curl-rich upsweep, Juliana sat on her bed and chatted on her cell phone with her great-aunt Katrina.

"The painting was *what?*" the elderly woman said.

"Auntie, please calm down. Don't make yourself sick." If that was indeed what was happening.

Aunt Katrina was known for using her advancing age to influence others, meaning that she was somewhat manipulative when she needed to be.

It didn't make Juliana love her less. But it did often put her on guard.

She could just about see her aunt in her favorite multicolored, polka-dotted housecoat, taking coffee on the porch as the birds chirped good morning to Parisville.

But she could also imagine an oncoming anxiety attack until her aunt said, "I'm as good as a girl twenty years younger, dear. But an explanation about the painting would be lovely."

Thank goodness. "There was some confusion about its

location, but Jiro Mori just called to tell me *Dream Rising* is on its way. I'll be negotiating for it soon."

"I only hope you get to it before that Cole boy does. I still can't believe they're there, too. How did that happen?"

"I don't know, but they've been searching for it just as much as you have."

Sasha, who was wearing a hotel-supplied cotton *yukata* and slippers, strolled by Juliana, making a "chatty-chat-chat" motion with her thumb and fingers.

Juliana held back a laugh and reached for her cup of green tea on the nightstand, sipping as Aunt Katrina waxed on in a sweet yet firm voice about how those Coles would do anything to shame the Thomsens again.

All the while, Juliana's body tingled in remembrance of her afternoon with one of "those Coles." She'd had two more orgasms in that love hotel, making it a long, hot, wonderful time.

So why couldn't they have just another few hours? One more night...?

"Auntie?" Juliana finally said, cutting into her relative's one-sided discussion. "Remember, it's expensive to talk on this phone."

"Of course. I get carried away."

Her aunt blew her a kiss over the line, and Juliana wondered how this affectionate woman who had tucked her into bed at night and held her when she'd cried about her parents had it in her to despise another family so much.

"Good luck to you, sweetie," she said.

"Thanks. Try to cope without me."

"Without our Girl Friday?" Aunt Katrina laughed—a full-throated show of mirth that had always made Juliana join in. "I'm trying, but being back at that bookstore just reminds me of how much cheesecake I liked to sneak during slow times and how much work piles up when I chat with the customers."

"Well, try harder." She smiled. "Bye, Auntie."

"Bye, dear."

Juliana hung up, put the phone in her purse, then stood, pressing her hands against her own *yukata*. Back at the love hotel, she'd dried her hair and shirt before returning, but her skirt had still been wet. She'd hidden it from Sasha, who'd been busy writing up her detailed notes about Atami when Juliana had arrived.

Since her roomie had been so involved with her work, Juliana had involved herself with her own business and phone calls, keeping her lips sealed about her afternoon, even though she was chomping at the bit to talk.

After all, telling her friend was like telling herself, right? Sasha would keep it under wraps, so it wouldn't be like letting the cat out of the bag.

Now, Sasha sighed as she dug through the drawers to which she'd transferred her clothes from the suitcase.

"Having a wardrobe crisis?" Juliana asked.

"There's no iron in the room, so I'm looking for my black jersey dress, which doesn't wrinkle too badly." She stood, looked around. "Did I even pack it?"

"I didn't see it in the closet."

Sasha knocked the drawer closed with her hip. Juliana could tell she was frustrated about more than a dress.

She was ready to talk about Chad. Finally.

So Juliana waited and, sure enough, Sasha crossed her arms over her chest and sighed again—but this one had a tremble to it.

"I left him in the dust at the castle, Jules," she said. "All afternoon, I've been working like a demon to forget. But I can't. My pride got the better of me. So did...I guess fear of failing twice, also."

"What did he say to you?"

"Nothing bad. It was all...good. I was tempted to give in to him again, because I think it's still there for him, too, the affection. The hope." A slight smile lifted the corners of Sasha's mouth, as if she were remembering, but then it dissipated. "I told him I couldn't try again. I don't have the strength, and..." Sasha shook her head. "I just don't have the strength to go through it if it doesn't work out."

"Yes, you do." Juliana came over to rest a hand on her friend's arm. "You're stronger than anyone I know."

Even Juliana herself.

But she was working on changing that.

"Thanks for saying so." As if that covered everything, Sasha went about opening another drawer, searching through it. Then she paused, glancing back at Juliana. "Really, Jules. Thank you for believing that."

She's drained to almost empty, Juliana thought, recalling the spark she'd seen in Sasha's eyes earlier, at the harbor.

That spark was gone again.

She wanted her friend to have the time of her life here, not the worst of it. Still, she knew when done was done, and if Sasha wanted to explore her feelings, she'd do so tonight over dinner or drinks.

So that was it, as far as Chad went.

But Juliana knew what would cheer up Sasha now, what would make her forget about Chad a little more so that it wouldn't be so hard to delve into a deeper conversation about him later.

"So, guess what?" Juliana asked, her voice light.

Sasha stopped searching the drawers, interest drawn on her face. "Why do I have a bad feeling about that question?"

Juliana put on an innocent expression. "About something *I* did?"

"Yes, you scamp." Sasha sat on her bed, giving Juliana a tell-me glance. "Go on."

Her heart started to pound. "This afternoon, I wasn't shopping. I was…well, scoping out some possible research for your book. You know how you were interested in the love hotels?"

Juliana let that sink in.

It took a few moments. Then Sasha grinned. "No, you didn't."

Good—it looked like she'd put Chad behind her…for now.

"Oh, I did," Juliana said. "Several times, in fact."

"With Tristan Cole?"

"No, with 'The Locomotion' guy from the ramen house. *Yes,* with Tristan."

Admitting it brought a fever to her, a bout of phantom caresses that she kept reliving over and over again.

Sasha's mouth gaped.

Juliana shrugged. "I'll give you my notes for that research now if you want."

Her friend brushed aside the joke. "Tristan. Cole."

Even his name—the forbidden syllables of it—got her motor started. "Tristan—" her belly purred "—Cole."

Sasha tucked her knees under her on the mattress, leaning forward. "So…?"

Seeing her friend's shining eyes, Juliana thought her work for tonight was done.

But the small hammer of desire that kept tap, tap, tapping into her proved that she wasn't nearly done with the man who'd sent her to heaven and back today.

6

THE NEXT MORNING, Sasha woke up before Juliana, and she tried her best to keep quiet as she went about preparing for the coming day.

It had been an enjoyable night in the Roppongi District, where they'd talked more about Tristan over dinner at a jazzy French restaurant, which Sasha had been overjoyed to find in the middle of Japan. Then jet lag had caught up, and they'd forsaken any research in the sexy bars and clubs Sasha had meant to visit in favor of turning in early at the hotel, thinking they'd make up for it today and tonight.

Or maybe she was avoiding it, which she could hardly afford to do. Not for the first time, she wondered if she'd bitten off more than she could chew with this topic, and if it could be that she was afraid to face it.

At any rate, Sasha thought, while securing her hair in its ponytail, she had the luxury of staying in Japan longer than Juliana, so there was no rush. Maybe she would even hire a private guide after her friend went home and Sasha had felt her way around the city a bit more.

By the time Juliana rolled out of bed, Sasha had already prepared the tea provided by the hotel and was surfing the

Internet for some of those love hotels her friend had talked about. She meant to explore those in the book, but now she was extra curious.

Yet while she searched, a keen wistfulness invaded her. Love hotels weren't for single people....

She brushed the thought aside, wondering instead if she *could* check into love-hotel rooms by herself, or if she should bring Juliana. But if she did that, would they have to go somewhere that accepted same-sex couples, since that's how it would look with her friend along?

Needing a stretch, she stood, then opened the curtains to a rain-splattered view of Shinjuku Gyoen Park. Late last night, the weather had turned, bringing gray skies with it.

Gray skies. Lonely.

Face it, Sasha thought. *Chad's in town and you wish you were with him right now.*

That's the reason she wasn't talking about it to Juliana: because she just might break down if she told her friend how badly she'd wanted to encourage Chad back at Atami Castle. How hard it'd been to stick to her guns and leave him behind while she moved forward.

So why did it feel as though she was marking time in the same place?

Juliana finished getting ready, choosing to wear pants with a sleeveless, collared linen top. Sasha's clothing was similar, right down to the light raincoat she'd been warned to pack. They were headed for Harajuku, where they wanted to spend Juliana's unexpected day off checking out the trendy shops and the hip youth who'd brought media attention to the area by loitering around in splashy over-the-top costumes.

Sasha and Juliana ended up doing just that, not arriving back at their hotel until nearly dusk, their arms loaded mainly with items from a vintage store that sold old kimono and 1950s wear.

It'd been too hard to resist shopping, and between that and lunch, Sasha had run out of research time.

Or, maybe it was that avoidance thing again, because thinking of all the hot romance she was supposed to be uncovering only whipped up Chad's blue gaze, Chad's familiar scent...

Chad, Chad, Chad.

Juliana dropped her last package on her bed. "Tell me when I'm going to wear a used kimono?"

"It's a perfect souvenir."

"A pretty expensive one, too, even though it's a simple creation. But it kept calling to me. 'Buy me. Have me. I'm beautiful.'"

Laughing, Sasha started for her computer, then noticed the message light on the phone flashing.

Juliana saw it at the same time, then sent a grin to Sasha before picking up the handset and accessing the message.

Tristan. Juliana was obviously hoping it was him.

And, at first, Sasha thought it was, because her friend's smile only got dreamier. But then after Juliana hung up and dialed another number, saying a sultry "Hi" to the person on the other end, she gradually angled away from Sasha, as if wanting to hide her expression as she "mmm-hmm"ed, "oh-I'm-not-sure"ed then finally said, "Okay, we'll give it a try in a half hour."

When she ultimately set down the phone, she was hard to read.

"What's up?" Sasha asked.

Juliana's blond brows were slightly furrowed, but then they straightened.

"What do you say we put on our dinner clothes and then grab a drink in the lobby?" she asked. "Just a quick one."

"Is Tristan meeting you there?"

"I suppose you could say that." She made for the clothing drawers.

"Juliana."

She turned around, a guilty cast to her expression that Sasha assumed was due to the whole Tristan affair.

"Just get dressed in snappy time, all right?" Juliana said, going about her business again. "Then we'll have our drink and get on with our plans."

"But—"

"Nope." Juliana held up a finger. "Trust me, Sash. I may seem cryptic right now, but it's going to be a great night."

Rather intrigued, Sasha went along with her, slipping into a modest yet stylish maroon sheath with capped sleeves, then pinning up her hair. Juliana chose a light-blue, summery dress.

They went downstairs to the lobby, and Juliana headed for a grouping of chairs underneath some chandeliers where one person was already sitting, his back to them.

Just one man with wavy, sandy hair...

Heart crashing to her stomach, Sasha turned away from Chad to face Juliana. "What's going on?"

Now her friend looked *really* guilty. "If you want to head straight out the door with me, then do it, and no one is going to fault you for it. But I have the feeling that you'd truly rather stay here. And you might not want to thank me now for this kick in the bustle, but I know you. You regret what didn't happen at the castle yesterday." Juliana paused. "But here's another chance."

Sasha didn't know how to respond. *You're right, Juliana, I haven't been able to stop wishing I'd reacted differently.* Or maybe a better option would be: *You and Tristan should just keep to your love hotels and let me do my own thing.*

There was that pride that had taken her over yesterday, almost ruining everything.

Juliana cocked her head, her gaze sad. "I only want you to be happy."

Now Sasha's heart slipped down to the floor.

This time, answering was easy, even if her throat was tight. "I know you want that."

She glanced back at the man in the chair, and it seemed as if everything were zeroing in on Chad: the light spearing toward him, the wood in the room closing in around him to make him the one, the only focal point.

Juliana was still talking in a rush of apologetic words. "That message on the phone? It was Tristan. He asked me to call him at his hotel, and at first I thought…*hoped*…he was asking me because he wanted to see me again. And he did want that, Sasha, but he also told me that Chad wanted to see you, even if it was just for a drink, and would it be okay for him to come over here? I told him yes, and I didn't tell you anything at first because I wanted to get your donkey-stubborn self in the same room with Chad before you made up your mind."

Sasha couldn't stop gazing at him—the man she'd missed with every passing minute, the man who'd broken her heart.

"Sasha?"

She tore her attention away from her ex, feeling as if part of her were being ripped, too.

Juliana put a hand on Sasha's arm. "Maybe we should just go to those clubs tonight. We'll paint the town red. Just tell me and it's as good as done."

Juliana's heartfelt plea finally registered with Sasha, and she grabbed her friend's hand, squeezing it.

She *did* want this, so badly it was chipping away at her.

But…scared. She was so damned scared that she'd experience more shattering truths—that they would come to a dead end again and it would hurt more than ever.

"It's just a drink," Juliana said. "That's all."

Only a drink.

Sasha glanced at Chad again, but her heart had already decided.

"What I have to talk to him about is going to take more than a drink," Sasha said. "I don't want to ruin your night."

"Then if you think this'll take a while," Juliana said, "I can make longer plans."

When Sasha glanced at her friend, she found Juliana looking off to the side of the lobby, near the concierge's desk, where a man dressed in a burgundy long-sleeved shirt and dark pants was waiting, nearly camouflaged by a crowd of Western businesspeople.

Juliana glanced back, her eyes full of desire. Full of yearning.

"Go," Sasha said, releasing her friend's hand. It felt as

if she were giving up a lifeline, coming to float and bob on her own.

Juliana smiled, whispered, "Good luck," then moved to where Tristan was, and Sasha felt as if she'd been set adrift.

But when she turned to see Chad waiting so patiently for her, she took a deep breath and dove in.

FROM BEHIND THE GROUP of businesspeople, Tristan watched Juliana approach, his pulse swatting at him as he recalled yesterday and how she'd left him to toss and turn last night, unable to stop thinking about her.

But now, here she was in a Wonderland-blue dress that clung to her waist, her hips. She'd worn her hair long again, and he wanted to damn all the hands-off customs in this country and slide his fingers through it as she came to stand in front of him, looking as pleased as pie.

"Phase One complete," she said, referring to Chad, Sasha and the setup Tristan had facilitated based on the drink-fueled talk he'd had with his cousin last night over room service. But neither he nor Juliana glanced over at the star-crossed couple.

He couldn't bring himself to look away from *her.*

A blush consumed her, and he knew she was remembering the waterfall, the pool, the bed in the love hotel, too.

The few hours they'd had together that he was trying to stretch into the here and now.

He skimmed a finger oh-so-subtly over her forearm, and she bit her bottom lip.

"Chad has big plans," Tristan said. "I'm glad that Sasha's giving him a shot."

"Thank goodness. She can't hide that she's been thinking about him ever since yesterday."

She was talking about Sasha, but Juliana's eyes told Tristan that she was thinking of herself, as well. That she'd run their tryst through her mind a million times in an attempt to experience every thrill again.

One of the businesspeople next to them, a suited man with receding reddish hair, addressed Tristan. "So you want to come with us then?"

Juliana looked at Tristan, clearly not expecting that he'd been over here making small talk with people as he waited for her.

He did a one-shoulder shrug—*I'm not* that *anti-social*—then introduced the group. They were a computer crew from the States who were in Tokyo to observe and learn from a major software company.

The lone woman amongst the four—a brunette named Caroline who wore her hair in a low ponytail—spoke to Juliana. "When we heard your boyfriend asking the concierge about things to do in the city, we butted in."

At the word *boyfriend,* Tristan and Juliana smiled at each other. They both knew better. But at the same time, something curved within Tristan, as if trying to change course.

He corrected it. They could have two nights together, and by the end of this one, it'd be over. The arrival of *Dream Rising* tomorrow guaranteed that, but common sense did, too.

The redheaded man, Charles, added, "We come to Tokyo a few times a year on extended trips, so we know our stuff. You'll like this snack bar we're going to. It's kind of a hole in the wall, and the *mama-san* who runs it always recognizes us."

When they'd mentioned it to Tristan earlier, it'd sounded perfect because the group could navigate the language and customs. Besides, Tristan had wanted to take Juliana out, anyway, flaunt her in public, even for just a meal—something they wouldn't have the luxury of enjoying out in public when they got back home.

The blood in his veins almost growled in anticipation.

It would almost be an alternative present, he thought. This was how it could have been if they'd come out in the open with their relationship and stayed together.

So sue him if he was taking advantage of borrowed time. Later, they'd have plenty of opportunity to get back to the real present, alone again in their separate hotels, remembering what waited for them outside of their front doors back in Parisville.

They all exited the hotel and met the rainy evening together, Tristan holding an umbrella over both Juliana and him. Then the business group—the Fab Four, Tristan thought—brought them to a subway that stopped in Ebisu, where the bars and restaurants were piled on each other, advertised by boxy, lit signs that reminded Tristan of the "down" parts of a crossword puzzle.

Mysterious, rain-slicked, sexy. It was exactly the romance he knew Juliana would enjoy, and he longed to see that smile on her face.

Longed to know that he'd made her happy in the midst of their damned family feud.

In a quiet section of a paper-lantern-strewn alley, behind a door with white panels that only hinted at silhouettes and a female voice raised in song, they found their "snack bar."

The dark-wooded, smoky room wasn't crowded, boasting only two people besides the singing woman. All lounged at a bar while the floor seats waited to be filled.

When the *mama-san* greeted the Fab Four plus Tristan and Juliana, she did it as if they were the most important guests there.

She was middle-aged, dressed in a dark-blue-and-gray striped cotton kimono. After she led them to chairs positioned around a table, she knelt and made a sedate fuss over the Fab Four, chatting, then welcoming Tristan and Juliana, too. She took drink orders and rose to fetch small dishes of salad and popcorn.

Near them, a few TVs played generic footage of a rolling ocean while karaoke lyrics scrolled over the bottom. Yet Tristan wasn't watching that. He was all too aware of Juliana sitting next to him, his thigh against hers.

He leaned over to talk to her, his mouth near her ear so she could hear over the music. "Did you have to cancel big plans for the night?"

She shifted, whisking a few soft hairs against his lips. The gentle contact sent blades of hunger through him.

"No, I was glad you called." She moved even closer. "Really glad."

Tristan itched to reach over and bring her onto his lap, where she could straddle him, her sex to his cock....

One of the Fab Four—Daryl, a guy who kind of looked like Tommy Lee Jones—canted toward them, and Tristan got his act together.

"Careful what you order," the businessman said over

the finale of the Japanese rock ballad that the woman was singing. "The bill adds up."

Erik, the fourth member, loosened his pinstripe tie. "Even this—" he gestured toward the first round of food "—equals a cover charge."

The woman finished her tune, and everyone clapped with enthusiasm.

One of the other men at the bar took up the microphone and started in with "Blue Hawaii" in Japanese while the *mama-san* brought their drinks.

Juliana lifted her glass of plum wine and Tristan held his beer in one hand, relaxing against the back of his chair. They toasted each other, then sipped, never losing eye contact.

The visual flirtation sent a zing through him, and he drank a little more to keep himself occupied.

"So," Charles the redhead said over the music as the rest of the Four began thumbing through the book of song selections. "Is there anything in this great country you have your heart set on seeing?"

Yeah, Tristan thought. *Juliana with her clothes off again.*

"We're going to a *ryokan* tomorrow," she said.

"Ah, the Japanese-style inn," the other man said, smiling as if recalling a time there of his own. "You'll love it. It's a beautiful experience, but very involved. They even have instruction sheets in the room about how to stay at a *ryokan*."

"Everything is involved here," Juliana said on an airy note.

But when she glanced at Tristan, he saw a double meaning.

The feud *makes everything too involved.*

Tristan tightened his grip on the beer while Juliana

folded one leg over the other, toward him. His senses went nuts, dodging and attacking and generally making him regret his fanciful notions of romance and taking her on what would have to pass as the one and only date between them. Ever.

Maybe he should've just taken her to bed, as Terrence had done with Emelie during their days of indolent love-making and picture-painting.

Before they'd had to face reality with his engagement.

Before the world had gotten to them.

Juliana was speaking to Charles again. "If there's anything else I wish I could see, it'd be a geisha."

Tristan remembered her carrying around some book about geisha in school, remembered being curious about what might be going through Juliana's mind. So he'd looked the word up in one of Gramps's encyclopedias.

He recalled now a few details about the accomplished women who so smartly pleased men; they were artists and occasionally mistresses who had to quit their calling if they wished to marry.

"A geisha would really be a sight," Charles said, "if you're lucky enough to catch a glimpse of a true one. Genuine geisha places are normally closed to outsiders. You'd need to be invited by a Japanese *insider* who's familiar with them. The company we work with over here hosted quite a banquet last year, Tokyo geisha and all. I count myself lucky to have been there."

The *mama-san* knelt by the table again, telling the Fab Four that a man at the bar had requested them to sing.

Tickled by that—but not very surprised—the Four told her their selections.

Then Caroline explained what was going on. "When we first started coming to this snack bar, the *mama-san* was wary because we're foreigners. But they're used to us now. We even get requests from the locals since they like to hear us sing American tunes."

Tristan could see that; when Charles ripped into his sub-*American Idol* version of "Danger Zone" in English, the patrons loved it, clapping at the end as if Charles were a rock star.

Juliana and Tristan applauded with the group, and by the next round of drinks, the Four were so into their karaoke that it left the two of them pretty much alone.

"You going to sing?" Tristan asked.

Juliana emphatically shook her head, her eyes wide.

"Oh, come on." He grabbed a songbook and turned to the sliver of a section near the back with the English tunes. "Madonna? Spice Girls? Britney Spears?"

"No, no and hell no."

He put the book down. "Not even a little Beyoncé?"

She laughed with such spirit that she leaned her head back, and his belly seemed to tilt like a room that'd collapsed on one side.

What was *that* about? She wasn't naked. She hadn't even made a sassy innuendo about what they could be doing in a bed just as soon as they'd finished eating enough to give them energy for the rest of the night.

At the tail end of her laughter, she tucked her hair behind her ear.

Then she went silent altogether when she saw what must've been a stunning intensity in his gaze.

He looked at her. She looked at him.

He'd fallen for her a long time ago, but now, in a place where no one would care how he felt about her, he was free to admit that he'd always hoped for another chance.

And he had it right in front of him.

JULIANA FAINTLY HEARD Caroline launching into another *Top Gun* song in the background, but it was all white noise.

The only thing she could really process was Tristan, the way he was watching her, as if...

As if he was looking *into* her.

She glanced away from him, leaning forward to grab her wineglass so he couldn't see anything in her eyes— not the delight she'd felt when he'd joked about her singing. Not the moment of personal connection that had threatened to turn this sexual romp into something that couldn't go beyond that.

As she sipped from her glass—maybe *this* was what was making her so fuzzy, all the plum wine—she reminded herself of tomorrow's meeting at the *ryokan* for *Dream Rising,* then of having to go back home all too soon.

If only they were different people, she thought.

But...they weren't.

Besides, what if Tristan *were* some guy her family would adore? Would she even bring him home?

Or would she keep him to herself just because it would be a show of hidden rebellion that would make her feel powerful in some petty way in the face of her family's control?

All she knew was that Tristan made her weak—her limbs, her veins, her willpower.

And she didn't *want* to be the weaker part of anything, like a mistress who had to answer to a man, or a subordinate who kowtowed to a boss or—

Or Emelie, she thought.

The realization rang through her as she leaned back against the chair, bringing her eye-to-eye with Tristan.

Not that he was going to ask her to keep seeing him in Parisville, but if he did, she wouldn't be his version of Emelie—the woman who was desperately in love with a man, only to be cast off like a paintbrush that'd gotten too old to be used anymore.

What *would* she do from this point forward?

Should she keep seeing other men who *weren't* Tristan? Men who bored her and didn't have a prayer of living up to him?

Would she trade in the love from her family to be with him beyond this trip?

She wished Emelie and Terrence were around to give her advice, to tell her if they regretted not fighting for each other.

What had *really* gone on between the two of them, even beyond all the family legends? She only had a superficial account of Emelie's side of the story.

Maybe there was a way for Juliana to find out....

"Know what might be interesting?" she asked Tristan, peering into his gray eyes. They were enough to talk her into just about anything.

Almost.

"What?" he said softly.

She could barely hear him, thanks to the music, but she could somehow feel his intimate tone feather through her.

"If you told me about what was in Terrence's journals," she said. "And I told you about Emelie's letters."

He sat up a little.

Of course. She'd almost forgotten that Tristan had let her go years ago, that he hadn't seemed all that invested in having her stay because he didn't want to make waves with his family, either.

He'd be loyal to them, just as she should be staying loyal to her own clan.

She straightened, too. "Okay, maybe there are certain places we shouldn't go with each other. That journal and those letters belong to our families, not just us. I know my relatives might go ballistic if I showed them to you."

"Right." He ran a hand through his thick hair, pushing it away from his face.

He looked conflicted, and she remembered how he'd told her that his father hadn't wanted him to jump all the way into the feud, becoming like his grandpa, who'd taken up Terrence's cause.

Was Tristan straddling some line right now between moving on from this feud or defending his family?

She tried not to get excited about the possibility.

"Let's pretend I never brought it up," she said. "It was a random idea, anyway."

"No." He rested his forearms on his thighs, his hair spilling back over his brow. "It was a good idea. If our families understood each other more, maybe..."

He clamped his mouth shut, and Juliana got the finger-in-light-socket feeling that he'd been about to say something neither of them should be saying to each other.

Maybe they would've had the courage to stand together

in front of their families, pursuing what they'd felt for each other back then.

Maybe it was time to end this now, before one of them did say the wrong thing. Before someone went *too* far when they'd already gone far enough.

The crowd, which had grown by three more Japanese customers within the past five minutes, applauded for Caroline as she ended her song, and she modestly gave them a wave.

Tristan slid Juliana a testing glance, and it pummeled her, mashing her common sense and leaving her bare with yearning for him.

She wanted him so badly, and what were they doing? Just sitting here talking about things that couldn't be changed.

There were only so many hours left before tomorrow, so why were they wasting time?

With more bravado than was good for her, she downed the last of her plum wine, feeling its warmth glide from her mouth, down her throat, to her gut then outward. Her desire was pointed, sharp, in need of easing.

"Ready?" she asked.

Passion making his gaze burn, he signaled to the *mama-san* to settle the bill.

7

THEY WENT BACK to his hotel because he had his own room.

And that suited him just fine, Tristan thought as Juliana retreated to the bathroom to "slip into something more comfortable," and out of her damp clothes; the rain had started coming down at a quickened angle, aiming itself under their umbrella on the walk back from the subway.

Meanwhile, he put on a pair of dark-gray sweatpants, then opened the bottles of green tea they'd purchased from one of the many vending machines—which sold everything from beverages to cigarettes to manga—on the way back because Juliana had said she had a hankering for the drink.

Imagine—him indulging her. His grandfather would throw a fit. And with all her talk about sharing Terrence's and Emelie's journals and letters, the notion swerved real close to the bone.

It'd snapped this fantasy time with Juliana in two, because he'd realized the seriousness of what they were doing. There'd never be family dinners, Christmas with the relatives…normal things that normal people did with those they loved.

But he didn't want to give Juliana up. The mere thought sent a jag through him.

So what was there to do? Have her as a secret mistress—just like Emelie had been to Terrence?

Discomfited, he picked up the tea and a hotel mug, preparing to pour the beverage. Juliana deserved better, although there didn't seem to be another option—*if* she was even open to extending this into...

What?

An actual relationship?

Tristan realized that, beyond all his dates, he'd never really had a commitment to a woman, maybe because he *had* been waiting around for Juliana.

She emerged from the bathroom in a hotel-supplied cotton robe, and all Tristan's motor skills came to a grinding halt.

Just being in the same space as she was...it slayed him. Her eyes and skin and lips all combined to hit a bull's-eye that only she exposed in him.

He remained there, holding the bottle, not pouring a drop, merely watching her while he could.

She was glancing around the room: the light walls and upholstery, the space-age-looking desk and chair by a window that showcased a rain-beaded night view of the Tokyo skyline.

Then her gaze skimmed the bed, and she smiled, completely assassinating him.

He struggled to get his cool back.

"Too bad," he said, "that the hotel doesn't have a silk kimono on hand for you to wear instead of that plain thing."

She fingered the cotton. "I bought one today. A kimono.

Not silk, just synthetic, but I still spent way too much money. I went a little bonkers on other souvenirs, too, for the family."

"Can't get around that." He pointed with the tea bottle to a nearby pile of shopping bags he'd dumped in a corner by his suitcase. "Chad and I got the souvenir-hunting over with this afternoon. We'd never hear the end of it from my aunts and cousins if we came home empty-handed, so we cleared some shelves."

He didn't know why it was, but even the most regular of topics had always engaged Juliana, and that always made conversation much more involving, even while relaxing in his car and staring out at the canyon where he'd taken her a few times that summer.

"What'd you buy for them?" she asked.

"You can take a gander."

She did, going to one bag and peering inside at the wooden dolls, carved cedar blocks and bamboo fans.

She extracted one of the latter and spread it, revealing a blossom-embroidered curve of red silk. Then she fluttered it in front of her face while batting her eyelashes at him.

His heart did a rogue flip, making him all hers once again.

"Just like a geisha, as you were talking about earlier," he said, finally pouring that damned tea into its mug. "You could be one of them with the way you're working that fan."

"Geisha," she said, as if putting the word through the dream factory of her mind. She sighed. "A long time ago I was on a kick about them. I went on mental benders about lots of things—Egypt, medieval Europe, ghost-hunting... In high school I'd spend days combing through the libraries and the used-book section of our store, grabbing any story I could find about all of them."

"I remember," he said.

She seemed surprised, then pleased. "You paid that much attention, even before we got together?"

"You knew that."

"No, you never told me. You'd said you were always aware of me, but... Heck, thinking about you keeping an eye on me in the halls and remembering the books I read... That's different."

"You had to know how crazy I was about you. That I wasn't just sweet-talking you, Juliana."

She took a step nearer to him, then set the fan against his bare arm. A flock of shivers swept over his skin, then dove below, digging and burrowing on the way to his core.

"How crazy were you about me?" she asked, smiling a little as she traveled the fan from his arm to his chest.

"Crazy enough to picture you as *my* geisha back then."

That seemed to inject some of that pesky reality into the moment, and she traced the fan back to his arm.

"Are you asking if I'll be your geisha now?"

He used his finger to tip her chin, making her look into his eyes.

But before he could say anything else, she stepped away from him, and he got the feeling that she was trying to keep everything on rendezvous footing, that she didn't want to get serious during this one night they had left.

"I read in my guidebooks that the geisha are different

all over Japan," she said, inspecting the fan, "but unfailingly, a *real* geisha isn't a mere sexual object."

"I know—they're not prostitutes or sex slaves." He set down the tea mug. "It's hard to say what they are, because their lives are complex. Westerners have a perception that they exist just to please men, but it sounds like they actually know how to *make* men think that their world revolves around them instead. As they get older, the successful ones can have financial independence and respect in their own worlds. They can even choose who they entertain, and if they want to take a patron—a *danna*—they do."

Like him, she must've read in her guidebooks about *danna,* and she must've known where he was going with this.

He couldn't even believe he was approaching the subject of mistresses. Hadn't he already decided that he wouldn't ask Juliana to live that kind of life with him?

Get a hold of yourself, he thought. What was he doing? Wasn't it too soon even to be thinking about a future?

But, deep inside, he knew that he'd waited long enough.

He came to stand in front of her, near the bed, and rested his hands on the sash of her robe.

"Geisha could be mistresses," she said. "But if they wanted to stay with the lives they'd trained so hard for, they wouldn't get married. You can't be a geisha and a wife at the same time. It would ruin their purpose—the reason men come to them in the first place."

"To get away from the real world." Just as the two of *them* had been doing.

She could only be his geisha for the time being, no matter how long he wanted her.

Juliana sketched the fan down his chest, stopping just above his sweats' drawstring, and the shivers below his skin turned to tremors.

"I couldn't ever be a mistress," she said. "I can't ever be an Emelie."

Something inside his chest seemed to crumble. But why? Asking her to live in secrecy would've been cowardly. He didn't want that for her.

Then again, wouldn't it be just as cowardly to go back to his garage when they got home and resumed a life of could-have-been?

She closed the fan, then placed it on the nearby desk, and he had no idea where they stood with each other as the rain tapped on the window.

Her chest rose and fell, as if she were controlling her breathing, trying to tame the pace of it.

Then, as if she'd made some choice right here, right now, she stood on her tiptoes, sliding her hands to the back of his neck, where she brushed her fingers, creating the shape of a *W*.

The butterfly sensation tore him up, and his blood tumbled to his groin, pumping, insistent.

And when she spoke, he knew that there'd be no more serious talk for now. That once they left his room, this would really be it, because tomorrow would bring the negotiations.

Tomorrow would burst this bubble of fantasy they'd managed to build around themselves—temporary and fragile and made to be broken.

"At their napes," she whispered as she pressed her fingers to the back of his neck, "the geisha leave the skin bare of pale makeup, creating a W or a V." She retraced the shape. "I read that the naked skin emphasizes the erotic slope back here."

Her touch was too much, and as she lowered from her tiptoes, he used the leverage to pull at her robe ties. The cotton whisked as it came undone.

"And underneath the kimono?" he asked, his tone strained, because it didn't help to be talking about this. Not this.

"No underpants." Her robe slumped open as she added, "They want to avoid panty lines, so they wear a thin silk cloth instead."

The robe gaped all the way, revealing Juliana's pale, slim body.

And she wasn't wearing underpants, either.

Heartbeat churning, Tristan slid his hands inside the opening, his fingers poised at her waist, his thumbs brushing the sleek lines of her stomach.

She leaned back her head, as if losing her willpower, then gathered herself, facing front again, her lips parted.

He listened to the primal beat of his blood, gave in to it.

Surrendered to the fantasy before it disappeared altogether.

A MISTRESS? Juliana thought.

Just like Emelie, who'd gotten her heart and spirit crushed because she wouldn't settle for being one after the man she'd loved decided to marry "properly"?

Was that all Tristan believed she could be, too?

As she took in the fervor in Tristan's gaze while he traced his fingers up to guide her robe over her shoulders then down her arms, she couldn't forget any of it.

But what other option would they have back in Paris-ville?

Tristan had swept her away here in Japan, even during the few hours they'd been together, and she knew in her heart that he could offer so much more. He was still the boy who'd talked about his dreams of owning a big vintage-car business one day—large enough to give him some independence. He was the same Tristan Cole she'd been smitten with, and this intimacy made her feel there was even more to come.

Yet how could Tristan and Juliana just ignore all the history and ill will between their families?

The robe deserted her body, rustling to the floor while the rain continued to knock softly at the window like a reminder.

Enjoy it while you can....

He held one of her hands as he led her to the bed and climbed onto it. Then, with his back against the high, smooth wooden headboard, he pulled her to him, her spine to his muscled chest, his legs bent on either side of her.

He'd positioned them so that they were directly in front of a vanity mirror near the television, and in its reflection, she saw herself, pale and naked, cradled.

Blood throbbed between her legs.

Coasting her hair back from her face, he whispered into her ear. "What're we going to do?"

Tristan rested one hand on her belly, tracing his fingers over it, creating a dangerous, swirling heat.

She winced, already under his spell. "For right now, just keep going."

He left his mouth against her, and she could almost feel his disappointment.

But what did he want her to do? Come up with some kind of plan that would magically please everyone?

She'd been a people-pleaser for her family, and it'd robbed her of Tristan in high school. It'd taken her from the tour business she'd hoped to raise to great heights someday.

She was tired of pleasing others.

When he insinuated his hand between her legs, she opened for him, intent on making this about what she wanted now. At least for the time being.

He slipped a finger between her already damp folds, then pressed on her clit, and she rolled her head to the side, pressure rising inside her like a roaring furnace.

Yet the guilt was still there, too. Although she'd decided to brush it aside, it wouldn't leave.

Even so, her heartbeat was choppy, and she felt every *ba-bump* echoing through her body, her center.

He slowly worked her with his fingers, gently seeking a way to bring her to the heights of passion. And he liked it as much as she did; she knew because she could feel him getting hard through his sweatpants.

"Homecoming," he murmured.

Her mind was so fuzzy that she didn't register what he'd said at first. "Homecoming?"

She sounded drunk—on him.

He swept his fingers around her, over her…then into her.

She gasped, her body arcing, and without thinking, she laid one of her hands over his, urging him on.

"Sophomore year," he said, his mouth against her ear. "You went with Pete Stosser, and you wore a blue dress that made you look like a princess. That was the first time I really wanted you. My crush turned into something a man—not a boy—would feel for any woman."

She got wetter as the nostalgia flowed through her, down and down. "I didn't know you were even there."

He slid his fingers in, out, wet and slow, and her clit went so stiff that she moaned, thinking it could never be assuaged.

By this time, his voice sounded like a growl in her ear, his mouth gnawing at her lobe as he spoke. "I didn't stay for long, but the more I did, the more I wanted to come up to you, show you what I tried to hide until that night we finally got together."

He thrust up into her, and she groaned, golden agony rising even higher.

The pressure... It was unbearable.

But so was the thought of giving all of herself to him when she should be holding back.

Yet she couldn't. Wouldn't.

Not until she had to.

Short of breath, she gripped his wrist, pulled his hand away from her and got to all fours, facing him while crawling backward, her hair over half her face.

Then she grabbed at his sweats, tugged, brought them over his waistline, over the trail of hair that started at his belly.

Just looking at it made Juliana's sex clench.

And when she looked into his gaze, she saw that he was about to come unhinged, too.

Before she knew what was happening, he'd sprung away from the headboard to gather her against his hard chest, her breasts smashed against him as they fought for breath, face-to-face.

He smiled against her mouth, lethal, taunting. "What's going through your head, Juliana?"

"Having you inside me again."

He smoothed a hand over her rear, and she closed her eyes without even knowing it.

"Is that all?" he continued.

No. There was so much more—so much that she couldn't imagine facing.

Instead she said, "Yes—"

As he stroked under the cheek of her ass, she groaned.

He spoke, more serious than ever.

"I'm thinking of more than just sex, too," he said.

But they shouldn't be thinking that way, she wanted to tell him as he rubbed his finger back and forth through her slit. She didn't want to repeat Emelie and Terrence's heartbreak, because if there was one thing history had taught them, it was that love could be unforgiving.

Then Tristan did something that suspended Juliana's heartbeat.

Tenderly, he eased her to the mattress, looking into her eyes the entire way, shattering all her thoughts until nothing made sense at all.

He touched his knuckle to her clit, adding pressure, and she bucked.

"Tell me what's going to happen from now on," he said, his tone scratchy.

There was a need in him—a raw openness.

A flare of panic flashed through Juliana as he ground those knuckles against her, and she swiveled her hips, bracing one arm over her head.

"Tell me, Juliana," he repeated.

"Why?" she asked on a gasp. "Nothing can happen."

"Are you so sure about that?"

He removed his fingers from her, then went back on his haunches to strip off his sweats. Then he came back to her, stretching out his legs and maneuvering her onto his lap so that they both faced the mirror again.

"Are you so sure," he said, "that you can go without this now that you know you can have it?"

She was sitting on his thighs, her sex wet against his flesh as he held her by the hips, and she knew what was coming next.

Her clit pounded, ready, slippery for him.

She took the initiative, leaning forward, bracing her hands on his legs, then hovering over his erection until it nudged at her.

Moaning in blissful anguish, he gripped her harder, and she sat on his arousal, let it slide into her, making her cry out. In the mirror, she saw the slick, thick root of his cock in her, and the sight added even more pressure to her escalating passion.

This doesn't have to be the last time, she thought, circling her hips, taking him in as deeply as she could while she leaned forward for leverage, pushing, working.

You could have this every night if you just had the guts.

It felt as if blinding steam was hissing in her belly, rising, expanding, and she lowered her head, unable to watch in the mirror anymore because it revealed everything.

Her ecstasy.

Her emotions, laid bare for a man she couldn't have.

But...no. No emotions, she thought, the steam beginning to knock around inside of her till she felt like a container about to blow. No...

Out of sheer desperation, she slid off him, bending down to his cock and taking it into her mouth to lave him and bring him to a climax that would keep him happy with what they had now.

She sucked, caressed, slowly yet emphatically showing him how she felt without letting it go beyond that until he came to a shuddering series of releases. Then, gradually, as she swallowed, pressing her hand against her sex, trying to make the ache go away, his breathing evened out.

While he leveled off, she nuzzled up next to him, pushing her own lust down and resting her head against his chest, just for a few moments.

Just until she forced herself to kiss him goodbye and leave this affair that had always been stamped with an expiration date.

8

CHAD AND SASHA had spent about a half hour at the hotel bar, talking around and around what they really needed to say, but Chad hadn't pushed it.

Not even once, although he'd gotten a strong feeling that Sasha had a lot on her mind, and she would get around to telling him all about it in her own time.

So, as he'd waited, she'd talked about her research, laughing almost shyly when she'd admitted that it was supposed to center around "woo-woo" things to do around Tokyo. He'd been surprised to hear that, too, based on how Sasha used to be.

Exotic and erotic?

She'd gone on to explain that she was really behind in her endeavors, so she'd have to start hitting hot-stuff establishments soon.

And that's when Chad finally sucked it up and risked suggesting that he could go out with her tonight if she wanted, just so she would have company in a country she was still hesitant to explore on her own.

The last thing he expected was for her to accept his offer without even a pause.

But was that because she needed to get her book going?

Or because it was an excuse to be with him?

Now, as they wandered a silent, rain-sheened neighborhood away from the more touristy section of Roppongi, Chad couldn't stop hoping it was the second option.

He'd picked the most romantic bar he could find in the guidebook, and the hushed streets made him think of a topsy-turvy edition of *Singing in the Rain,* when Gene Kelly had danced over the wet sidewalks, in love and wanting to announce it from here to there.

Chad glanced at the paper where the hotel concierge had written directions in the artful symbols of his language, followed by a translation in English. Chad had then shown the directions to their cab driver, who'd dropped them off here and offered what were probably more directions in Japanese.

Not that this had helped, but it had been a nice gesture.

Chad had thought bringing Sasha to the fringes of the Roppongi District was a decent idea, because from what she'd said over their cocktails, he knew it would feel fairly familiar and comfortable to her; she'd mentioned that she and Juliana had come to the tourist-heavy district last night, and she'd intended to return in order to check out more of the nightlife.

Rain popped on Chad's umbrella, sounding a lot like Gene Kelly's shoes. "The bar should be close."

Sasha, under the cover of her own umbrella, was inspecting the upscale homes around them, where BMWs were parked in Beverly Hills–type affluence.

"I'm not in a hurry," she said, smiling. Her serene expression went well with the surrounding foliage nodding under the raindrops, the slants of concrete architecture sloping in graceful angles.

Chad had noticed that she seemed far more relaxed tonight than she'd been at the castle, as if she'd thought things out in her complex Sasha way and she'd come to some kind of decision.

Maybe, just maybe, meeting him for that drink had been a big first step for her?

His veins tightened as he wondered what the next step might be.

Then the next.

His heart bumped in his chest while he took a long look around for any sign of the bar. The concierge had said in private to Chad that the best ones around these parts—the most romantic—were nearly hidden.

That they were behind closed doors.

And Chad was going to win Sasha back one bit at a time with all the romance he could muster. Last night, while he had brainstormed with Tristan during a beer-addled haze, everything had become crystal-clear: he needed to show the love of his life that she was more important to him than anything—work, family entanglements...pride.

Because that's one of the reasons they'd broken up, Chad had admitted. He'd been threatened by where her job might take her, and he'd been too proud to deal with it in the way a man should have.

He'd also been wounded by what he'd taken to be her lack of trust in him, her guarded feelings.

But he was damned sure going to try harder—starting now—to encourage her to bring those feelings out. He would wine and dine her until she couldn't help but sing in the rain with him.

If he was singing after tonight, that was.

He was beginning to think that Japan itself was like Sasha—sedate and ordered on the outside, but with passion boiling underneath all the customs, in a shadow world.

As he and Sasha wandered, they came to a door nestled below street level, at the bottom of some stairs that were nearly buried under a building.

He pointed to the door, and Sasha's smile only grew.

His heartbeat picked up, because the Sasha he'd known before would have opted for something less murky.

Then again, the Sasha he'd known wouldn't have come to a country as seemingly distant, sleek and foreign as Japan, either. The fact that she had—and to write a book about hot stuff, to boot—struck him.

Was she making an effort to open up? He'd suspected so when she'd told him about her book, but little by little, she was beginning to prove it.

He didn't dare hope it was because their breakup had changed something within her.

"I don't know if it's the place we're looking for," he said, testing her to see how flexible she would be.

He watched her for a response and, for a moment, he wondered if he'd been wrong about her changing.

But then she headed for the stairs, and his pulse gave a leap.

"We'll never know unless we try to open it," she said.

The rain had let up, and as they descended, they both closed their umbrellas, shaking them out.

He gestured for her to try the door, hoping she'd see that he didn't have to take control a hundred percent of the time, that he knew she would always need the freedom to do things on her own and he would appreciate this about her.

If she could change, he sure as hell could, too.

Their gazes caught, stayed, and a rush of brutal warmth swamped him.

In her beautiful pale-blue eyes, he could see that she had gotten the message.

She knocked at the door, but there was no answer.

Then she tried the handle.

When she pulled the door open, neither of them moved for a moment, because what they found took the breath away with its very simplicity.

A black wall with an alcove where a vase-bound rose bloomed under the glow of a spotlight.

The flower reminded Chad of Sasha's skin's texture, the scent of it, and his insides contracted with the need to touch her.

But he knew that was a bad idea, so he propped his hand above Sasha's on the door to open it wider and ushered her inside.

Slowly, they walked around a corner to the bar itself, where they checked their coats and umbrellas while the scent of incense floated on the air.

He'd been looking for romance?

Well, this was it.

The place was all dark walls and mist, with a bar shining a mere line of light that suffused the faces of two bartenders. Their hair was slicked back, their torsos covered by white linen shirts and black vests, adding to the impression that this was a scene from a minimalist play, with only a couple of other people haunting the bar seats and the tables.

The other customers were foreigners, too, Chad noted. Wanderers just like him and Sasha.

The feeling of isolation made him feel closer to her. Them against this new country, this new world.

He pulled out a seat at the bar for her, and the bartender bowed to them. They bowed back, and Chad ordered champagne because he knew she liked it.

It was probably going to cost an arm and a leg, but he didn't care.

As the bartender fixed their drinks, Sasha spoke.

"Thank you," she said, her words just as simple as that flower by the entrance.

"For what?" he asked, trying not to move too fast by revealing how significantly even a word or two from her could still affect him.

"For finding a buried gem like this." The bartender slid cocktail napkins before them while Sasha brought a notebook out of her small purse. "And thank you for encouraging me to go out with you tonight."

He held on to what she'd said for a moment.

"I know," she said. "Quite a change from what I told you at the castle. But seeing you was a shock, Chad. I was defensive, and after I left, I was angry at how I handled the situation. Angry at how I reacted." She opened the notebook to a fresh page and took a pen out of her purse, as well.

Was that all she was going to say? She still seemed a little guarded. Not as much as before, but he could feel it just the same.

Just as he started to think that she was about to go remote on him again, she blew out a breath, as if she'd been holding it. "I've been working up to telling you that all night."

Music to Chad's ears.

But he didn't start celebrating. Not yet. Sasha was *still* in the slow process of unguarding herself.

As the bartender served them champagne in long flutes that flared at the top while bubbles shot up from the base, Sasha scribbled notes about their surroundings. The bartender added plates of aesthetically arranged cantaloupe and cherries.

Sasha touched the plate, then laughed.

"Fruit is funny?" Chad asked.

She started to shake her head, but seemed to think better of shutting him out. Instead, she made an obvious effort to look him in the eyes, and the pale-blue connection was a jolt to his system.

He'd never forgotten how beautiful those eyes were.

"I almost expected them to serve me parsley," she said.

He frowned at the odd statement.

"It's a joke," she added. "Unmarried women over the age of twenty-five in Japan are referred to as 'parsley.' Because that's what's left on the plate? Get it?"

Now he laughed, too. "The last thing I'd call you is a leftover."

Her smile was sweet, and it threw his heart right over.

"Juliana would be grateful to hear that, too." Then she glanced back at her notes. "Wherever she is, I mean."

Chad sipped his beverage, the taste superdry and definitely expensive. He'd stopped thinking about his and

Sasha's travel partners hours ago when Sasha had told him that her friend was under the weather and was going back up to the room for the night.

The thing was, when Chad had said goodbye to Tristan, he'd been in Juliana's hotel lobby....

His thoughts jerked back to the here and now as Sasha ate a piece of fruit and closed her eyes with a joyful moan.

He recalled nights in bed, him inside her...

"This cherry," she said. "It's amazing."

"The Japanese pay top dollar for their produce." He'd barely gotten the words out from his closing throat, but huzzah to him for managing it.

"I mean..." She finally opened her eyes. "Talk about appealing to the senses."

He paused in his next drink, because she was shooting him such a look of obvious lust for life—lust for *him?*— that it took him a moment to absorb it.

But there she was—the woman he'd always hoped to uncover. The one who moaned at the taste of a simple cherry or basked in the fizz of bubbles from champagne on her face.

His chest seemed to fold out, his heart catching the light he'd always seen in her but hadn't ever shone like this, under the low mist of a bar on the other side of the world.

Had it taken thousands of miles to finally get here?

"Maybe you can include the joys of eating their perfect, expensive fruit in your book," he said, still hardly daring to believe what was happening.

She toyed with the stem of her champagne flute. "Maybe."

She smiled faintly, took a sip, closed her eyes in pleasure again, and generally made Chad's temperature shoot through the roof.

Too soon to touch her, he thought, *to be a part of what she's feeling. Just wait.*

Even when she put down her flute, she kept hold of it, glancing around the bar.

"So many shadows," she said.

"It adds ambience."

"I'm not just talking about this bar, really." Her gaze searched his.

Here it was.

Chad wanted it… He didn't want it…

But he *did,* even if it was only closure.

"You can say anything to me, Sasha." He took a chance, touched her arm, then removed his hand and rested it on his thigh. "Anything."

She seemed to steady herself, then said, "If I were to be completely truthful with you about why we broke up, I'd have to say that part of it was because I felt overshadowed by your devotion to your job and to the whole Cole mystique. They're entwined, actually, and I was sure that they didn't leave much room for me or even a life of our own. Maybe that's why I hung back when I wish now I hadn't."

This was his chance to make up for everything. "I've thought a lot about that, too, and how it affected us. There's more to life than I used to believe, Sasha. There's *you.* And you're everything."

Her hand flew to her chest, over her heart. Her fingers seemed to cage it before she took them away.

"After we went our separate ways," she said, "I thought that proving I wasn't in love with you would make me stronger. I lived with that credo for months, and it's hard to let it go."

Chad looked at her hand, which she'd lightly fisted on the bar near her champagne.

Now. Now's the time.

Carefully, he eased his hand over hers.

She glanced down, watching how he covered her fingers.

Purposefully, he slipped his hand into hers, bringing them to an equal level on the bar.

As if acknowledging his efforts, she squeezed his fingers.

When he'd first heard that she was in Japan, he'd wanted to see her, but there'd also been a desperate need to know why they'd broken up, and *that* had driven him to go to the castle, too. After all, he hadn't been able to move on with his life during the limbolike months that followed her departure.

He'd even wondered if there was a part of him that had wanted to win her over again so he could tell himself that he wasn't the loser he'd felt like.

But as she slid her thumb over his, he knew this was only about loving Sasha.

The bartender walked by, and they let go of each other in favor of holding their drinks, sipping from them. The fizzy liquid quenched a physical thirst, but it did nothing else but send bubbles to his head.

It must have done the same for Sasha, too.

"Maybe tonight," she said, "if you haven't got anything

else to do, you'd like to see a few more bars with me? For my research, I mean."

"I was hoping you'd ask."

"Good." She took another sip of champagne, then shot him a lively smile.

One he hadn't ever seen.

One that made him fall in love all over again.

"And," she continued in a lowered, hopeful voice, "maybe tomorrow you can even help me with some things that we don't have in America. Things I've been thinking about trying, and now that *you're* here…"

He agreed before she'd even finished.

THE NEXT MORNING, Tristan walked with Chad to Shinjuku Station, where a train was scheduled to leave in twenty minutes for Hakone and Jiro Mori's *ryokan,* where he would be staying the night.

People walked around them at a fast clip while he and his cousin stepped to the side, near a food kiosk, where they wouldn't be in the way of the masses.

Tristan set down his overnight bag, thinking it felt surprisingly heavy. But maybe that was only his thoughts, which had been weighing him down since Juliana had left him and his bed empty last night.

There'd been sex—great sex—but he'd messed up and asked for more.

Even now, he cursed himself, knowing he should've kept his mouth and his emotions shut tight. What had he been expecting, anyway? He'd gotten his curiosity about what could've been appeased.

He only wished…

Chad's voice interrupted. "You set for this?"

Tristan nodded, almost having forgotten that he had much bigger issues to deal with involving Juliana.

The painting.

His cousin was watching him closely through his glasses, but even that thoughtful inspection didn't make Chad seem any less like he was walking on air.

He and Sasha had made progress last night, so at least one of the cousins was going to leave this country happy.

"I'll keep in contact," Tristan said, hoping to avoid any questions from his cousin about his dark mood.

"You already know the cash ceiling on what we can spend on *Dream Rising,*" Chad reminded him.

"Yup."

"So give me a call when I need to start the finance machine rolling."

"Are you sure you don't want to be at the *ryokan* with me for this historic moment?"

Chad raised both his hands, as if to ward off the thought. "Let's remember that Jiro Mori didn't expressly invite me. I wouldn't want to be a rude barbarian and crash the party."

Tristan also knew that Chad planned to spend the day helping Sasha with her research, mending their relationship, and his cousin could see to his part in this family business here just as well as in Hakone.

"All right then," Tristan said, reaching out to shake Chad's hand before he picked up his bag.

But his cousin wasn't hoodwinked. "Just don't go into negotiations looking so glum."

"Who's glum?"

"Oh, come on," Chad said. "Like I don't know you have a thing for Juliana Thomsen."

A thing.

Hell, it'd gone way, way beyond that. It was "a thing" that'd gotten him maybe an hour of restless sleep last night, just as he'd had the night before. It was "a thing" that made him wonder if he could go back home without it.

Or if he would ever find this "thing" with anyone else again.

Tristan started to walk away, then paused. "Listen, I know that you're finally getting a fresh start with Sasha, and I'm glad for it. Believe me. I was only doing the same with Juliana."

Chad clearly didn't know what to say.

"I'm not going into details," Tristan added, "but it seems to me that we all deserve a second chance, no matter who it's with."

"I never knew—"

Tristan held up a finger. "And you're going to keep on never knowing. Got it, Chad?"

His cousin only assessed him, and Tristan didn't know if it was because Chad was wondering if Tristan was up to negotiating with Juliana Thomsen now.

As Tristan headed out, Chad stopped him.

"Take it from me—don't let what the family thinks sway you. I let that happen when Sasha left, but I thought *you* always knew better."

Tristan didn't move. "I didn't."

He'd lost her, just as he was losing her again. And it was because she obviously didn't want to pursue their "thing" anymore. It was just like the first time she'd left him behind.

Or maybe it was because he refused to lay his own feelings on the line.

"Well, then," Chad said, narrowing his eyes under glasses that'd obviously become rosier after last night's date with Sasha, "don't you think it's about time you started knowing better?"

Without another word, Chad walked off through the crowds with his hand in the air as a farewell, and Tristan realized that his cousin had started on his way forward with Sasha, with life.

And he was only going backward.

JULIANA AND SASHA had decided to grab some bakery snacks for Juliana's train ride, so they went to a department store near the station before departure.

As Juliana purchased a melon custard muffin and cheese-stuffed bread—Lord, she wished she'd discovered department-store bakeries to dull the sadness earlier—she listened to the clerk keep up a constant patter of conversation. At first, she thought the young, musical-voiced woman was gabbing with her coworkers. But Sasha told Juliana that she thought the clerk was actually detailing everything she was doing for Juliana, bringing customer service to a whole new level they weren't used to.

With their food wrapped, they took a quick tour of the store, where Juliana couldn't resist buying a gift bag that featured a cute bear with its arms in scare position while a darling cat waved hello.

"Bad Bear Versus Good Cat," the bag read, and Juliana

couldn't help loving how the Japanese seemed to adapt English words randomly for trains, products and even mottos on gift bags.

Truthfully, though, she'd hoped shopping would divert her from thinking about Tristan, but it didn't.

She was nervous about how they would react to each other today, during business, when they both knew their affair was over. Or, more to the point, she was anxious about how *she* would respond to him.

Even now, her blood was pistoning through her.

What had happened to the innocuous affair they'd started? What had happened to the time-in-a-bottle notion that she'd satisfy her curiosity and explore her sexuality and then be done with it?

"I suppose I should head back to the hotel before I meet Chad," Sasha said. "Want me to take your bear and cat with me so I can stow it in the room?"

Thanking her, Juliana handed her purchase over, noticing again how Sasha fairly glowed under the cleared weather. Her eyes were just as blue as the cloud-free sky.

"So you're taking Chad to love hotels today?" Juliana asked, trying to brush off the melancholy that was still dogging her. "This trip has already turned you around, baby."

"We're just going for look-sees."

"And what if…"

"Don't get ahead of things." They stopped at the commuter-choked entrance to the station. "We're just getting back on common ground. Anything more would be premature." Then Sasha sent her an unsure glance. "Don't you think?"

"I think you should do whatever feels right."

They smiled at each other, and even in that one small gesture, Juliana could see that her friend had truly shed most of the shell that had always kept her at a distance.

It cracked Juliana's heart, because it was almost as if *she* had taken that shell and slipped into it herself, with Tristan.

She'd always admired Sasha, especially after her friend had left Chad to chase her own dreams without anyone or anything to hold her back. Juliana had wanted the same independence but, like Sasha, she was finding that there was something missing.

The other woman took hold of Juliana's fingers. "Hey. You thinking about him again?"

"Always thinking."

Always staying in her role as Girl Friday, the family loyalist, even though she'd tried to slough it off for a few days.

But she hadn't even managed to do that, because here she was, away from him because she was *still* that Girl Friday.

Would she always be?

"Bye, Jules," Sasha said as she let go of Juliana's hand. "Good luck, okay? Call me if you need to."

"I will," Juliana said, having no intention of doing so as she watched Sasha walk away.

As always, she would handle this on her own, staying faithful to what she knew, putting everything else on the back burner for the bigger Thomsen picture because it was so much easier that way.

She turned around, heading for the trains, feeling as if she were going nowhere.

9

LIKE ATAMI, Hakone was a resort town known for its hot springs. But where the first location had the Adult Museum, the second had a view of Mount Fuji.

One was naughty, the other a nature-infused sister to Yellowstone.

When Tristan arrived in Hakone, he used the directions Jiro Mori had given him to take a very short taxi ride to the *ryokan,* which waited on the incline of the road, a traditional pagodaesque hotel under the bent sway of trees.

As he looked at it, his heart sank, mainly because it was the type of place you would take a woman for a weekend alone. He could easily imagine bringing Juliana here to hold each other for hours, shutting themselves away.

But that was the problem, wasn't it?

Shutting her away. Pretending that he hadn't fallen for her, keeping the greatest find of his life a secret from the family he also loved.

Last night, Juliana had left him as surely as she'd done all those years ago, and he hadn't the initiative to force the issue; he regretted it now.

If he'd asked her outright, instead of only hinting around at it to avoid being wounded by her yet again, would she have told him that she wished, more than anything, to come clean to their families?

He hadn't wanted to hear anything else, so he hadn't directly asked. Losing her the first time had done too much damage that was just coming to the surface, and he didn't need any more of it.

As Tristan looked at the sky, he noted that although the weather had cleared in Tokyo, it was rainy here. So he nixed his plans to take a walk around town before the negotiation, which was scheduled for a few hours later in the day.

Instead, he would relax inside, he thought as he arrived at the hotel's entrance. He had an interesting-looking book about the *yakuza* that he'd purchased while souvenir shopping, and he'd been meaning to start it anyway.

His body protested that sedate idea by tightening, reminding him that Juliana would be here, and instead of reading in his room, he could be with her.

Yeah, he thought. Like knocking on her room door would be that easy, now that the painting had arrived.

And now that the sex had somehow gotten more complicated.

When he entered the hotel, he was greeted by two women, each in a cotton kimono; the younger one retreated from the room while the older one warmly welcomed him in Japanese. Thanks to his basic language lessons, he understood her and responded in kind. As the younger woman returned with Jiro Mori, Tristan was shedding his work boots for slippers because wearing shoes inside a *ryokan* would be considered unrefined.

"Tristan-san," the art dealer said, bowing. He was

wearing a *yukata* and, even with his blue-streaked hair, he looked more traditional in this setting. "My first arrival. Your trip was smooth?"

"Yes, thank you." So Juliana wasn't here yet. The news made the surroundings fade a little.

"I made certain that you and Ms. Thomsen will be the only guests tonight. You'll have the run of the hot baths, along with everything else." Jiro thanked the women and motioned for Tristan to follow him. "Let me show you around."

He gave him the tour, including the baths, the communal restrooms and, last but hardly least, the arrestingly green, rain-jeweled gardens with their stone lanterns, rocks, streams and bamboo trees.

Each sight pierced Tristan, because all he could think of was Juliana here with him, breathing in the fresh air from the screened windows, watching the rain while he watched her.

Jiro led Tristan through the cedar halls and eventually brought him to his room. There, Jiro slid open the *shoji* door and bade his guest enter after they had doffed their slippers, which weren't to be worn on the *tatami* mats covering the floor.

"I'll be sending your personal maid to you," Jiro said, walking around in his socks, "but she doesn't speak English. I know you can get along a bit with your Japanese, but I thought I might answer any questions you might have before she gets here."

Jiro handed Tristan a tip sheet in English that explained how to stay in a *ryokan,* and it seemed like that would be enough to get him through the night.

When Tristan told Jiro as much, his host nodded, then finally got around to mentioning the reason they'd gathered here.

"At five o'clock," he said, "we'll meet downstairs for libations and business. Then we'll have a meal you'll never forget. And you can wear your *yukata,* even out of your room," Jiro added, motioning to his own robe. "You're here to relax, and if there's anything I can do for you, please don't hesitate to mention it."

At his smile, Tristan said, "Sounds great. I'm looking forward to all of it."

They bowed to each other, and his host departed, leaving Tristan to glance around the room, wondering where the most comfortable place to sit would be. A chair—which was really just a cushion with a straight back located on the floor at the level of a low, glass-topped table—wasn't his number one choice. But there were bamboo seats near a table that overlooked the garden.

Of course. There would be a garden, and it would *have* to smell like Juliana's hair.

Chest aching, he meandered over there, the view making him realize that his room was basically a bridge over the greenery.

The open window allowed in the scent of humid leaves and rain, a lazy fragrance that mixed with the room's own aroma of cedar and what smelled like straw from the mats. And as Tristan took in the room from this vantage point, he noted that the place was clean-lined and elegantly simple, with windows and screens featuring slim, angled wood designs over the white of glass or rice paper.

There was a tiny TV in the corner, a small safe, an old

phone. The tap of rain on leaves and the roof. The call of birds.

It was almost enough to make him forget.

His maid came, and she gestured for him to sit in the low chair while she poured green tea and offered a jellylike yellow candy wrapped in a leaf. She also had him fill out an English questionnaire about service preferences: things like when he wanted breakfast and if he liked to use chopsticks.

She showed him the *yukata* he was to wear, then left.

He drank his tea, listened to the rain, tried to read, took out his phone and toyed with the idea of touching base with his number one vintage-car client so they could meet tomorrow.

Yet after dithering for about an hour, he couldn't stand it, and he stole out of his room, not admitting to himself that he wanted to see if Juliana had arrived yet.

She had, and when he caught her in her own gray-and-white *yukata* wandering the halls, playing the curious tourist in a cryptic place, his breath caught in his chest.

She was looking out a screened window into a garden, an expression of such wistfulness on her face that it bent something inside him like a steel crowbar curved by heat out of its normally direct line.

Did everything about this place remind her that she could be enjoying the quiet with him, too?

"All settled?" he asked softly.

He hadn't wanted to startle her, but his voice seemed to have that effect anyway, making her suck in a breath as she glanced at him.

Her gaze made him think that maybe she *had* been thinking about him all this time.

"So what's your take on all this?" he asked, avoiding the tension that was so clearly hanging between them like a fog that it made his lungs heavy.

"My take?" She glanced at the garden again. "A place like this can sweep you away from just about everything else."

Just like the love hotel, the snack bar...his own room last night.

He was talking before he even knew what he was saying. "In a perfect world, I would've wanted to bring *you* here, just like a normal couple."

Okay. So he'd said it.

And he was damned glad he had.

She blushed, as if she'd been touched by his words.

Something within Tristan rose, up through his chest, pushing out.

But then she looked at the floor, and it was obvious that she was going to keep to the family hard line, come hell or high water.

"I can't, Tristan," she finally said. "I love my aunt—my whole family—too much. And even though I've told myself that I need to change, I'm not sure I could deal with the disappointment they'd..."

Her voice cracked, and all he wanted to do was go to her, hold her, tell her he felt the same way but, together, maybe they could convince their families that all this was wrong. That the feud had resulted in tragedy with Terrence and Emelie, and it didn't have to do so again.

But she walked away from the window before he could do it, then nodded her head to indicate that he should follow her down the hall.

To where? he thought, his pulse beginning to race—not necessarily because of what might physically happen if they went to her room.

It could've been just because he was going to be with her, near her, close enough for his senses to take her in until her scent, her *presence,* was absorbed into every part of him.

"I was hoping to find a section of the garden that was safe from the rain," she said, her voice whole again. She'd recovered. "But it's all in the open. I had this Victorian notion of looking over Emelie's letters outside because I thought communing with her might get me in the frame of mind to negotiate."

She put her hand on the sash of her *yukata,* where he noticed she'd stashed a bunch of copy-quality papers.

Emelie's letters, he mused, thinking of the copies of Terrence's journal pages that he was carrying in his own travel bag.

They came to his room first, so he silently invited her in.

When she paused, he wondered if maybe she'd only wanted to walk around with him, with no rendezvous involved.

But that would've meant that just being around him was enough for her, too.

His heartbeat doubled in time, and he tried to read her.

A moment passed, the seconds beating out in his chest until she smiled almost shyly and accepted his invitation to enter.

After shedding their slippers, they sat in the low chairs overlooking the garden, acting as if the humid awareness wasn't still surrounding them.

He didn't know how long he could carry this off without reaching across the table, just to touch her.

She took the papers out of her sash and laid them on the table, probably because sitting down made it uncomfortable to have them tucked against her body.

"Funny," she said, "but outside of what we shared after high school and now in the bedroom, I'm not sure I even know you that well."

That slammed him, because he knew she was right. "What do you want to know then?"

She shook her head, laughed a little. "Everything? Maybe how much you like your job? Maybe if you've ever been in love since we were young? We've skipped over all of that."

"Yeah, we did."

Their gazes held, just as they always did when they were in a room or an alley or anywhere together, and his adrenaline surged.

Okay then. He was willing to tell her everything if it would…

What?

What exactly did he want from her?

He continued. "Cars are what I've always done, ever since I was a kid. Finding heaps of metal with potential, fixing them until they gleam, selling them to someone who'll treasure them. It's peaceful, that job. It always has been. Keeps me out of trouble, too."

She smiled, and he wanted to tell her more.

"And about falling in love?" He fortified himself with a breath. "How could I when you set the standard, Juliana?"

She flinched, then blushed.

Had he gotten to her?

"It was just puppy love, Tristan," she finally said, and he could tell that she was trying hard to convince herself of that idea.

He wasn't sure that she was succeeding though.

"Maybe. But I always hoped that you might come around again one day—that we'd see each other and it'd be as if only an hour had gone by."

The rain kept popping away on the foliage, providing a wall of sound to cushion the pause.

When she next spoke, she did it quietly. "Me, too."

He'd barely heard her, and he hardly had time to respond before she added, "But, growing up, stories about Emelie and Terrence influenced me more than I'd ever admit. I was a sucker for a good romance, sure, but there was…something else. I knew their breakup was harsh—enough to start a feud, for heaven's sake—so I think, even subconsciously, I started protecting myself from having the same thing happen to me. I'm not sure I even realized it until I came over here and had enough room to myself to really sort through everything."

"What're you saying, Juliana?"

She blew out a breath. "When I left you for college, it wasn't an easy choice, but you didn't seem inclined to keep me there. I suppose I was protecting myself, the way Emelie should've done with Terrence. Maybe I even wanted to keep the memory of what we had for that one summer…" She seemed to lack the word to complete her thought.

Then her gaze went hazy and soft again when she found it.

"Pure," she said. "I wanted to keep it pure."

A dream, he thought. A story she could go back to time and again like the first part of Terrence and Emelie's.

Shaking her head, she added, "The two of us barely knew each other, even though we spent all that time together. There was never a guarantee that anything would've come out of kisses and stolen moments, anyway."

"I wanted you to stay."

It was only now, when she looked up at him, that he saw just how confused she was about all of this.

"Then why didn't you say so?" she asked.

Because he was fully aware of Terrence and Emelie, too? Because he thought that they would bring him and Juliana grief because of all the inescapable bitterness these two ancestors had handed down from generation to generation?

She rested her fingers on Emelie's letters. "Can you imagine going back home and dealing with the guilt? Our families would never let us forget, Tristan. We'd have to make a choice between us and them. There'd be no middle ground."

The room seemed to suck into itself.

A choice.

Would she be willing to make one now, unlike in the past?

She just kept her fingers on those letters, as if unwilling to let them go while she watched him, her gaze bared, a deeper violet than he'd ever seen in his life.

But what if she could move on and let go of what those letters symbolized?

At the same time, was he ready to turn his back on his duties?

He thought about his gramps—how he lay in his bed with a troubled frown, even in sleep. How Tristan had vowed to do anything to wipe it away and make the man who'd meant so much to him his whole life smile.

Yet Tristan also wanted Juliana. So badly it was tearing him apart.

Terrence and Emelie, he thought. Him and Juliana.

It hit him.

They were falling into a trap, just like their ancestors, and they weren't going to get out unless they confronted the pride that Terrence and Emelie had let ruin their own lives.

It had taken a trip here to learn this, to a world that couldn't have been more distant in miles and culture, a place that upended everything he was used to.

These nights spent hiding with the woman he wanted in private love-hotel rooms had finally forced Tristan to see clearly.

He got up, retrieved Terrence's pages from his bag, and brought them to her.

At first, Juliana just stared at him, as if she couldn't believe it. This gesture.

This grand statement he'd made without any words at all.

But then she raised her fingers from Emelie's pages, allowing Tristan to take them.

As the rain fell, they sat across from each other, reading together in silence, yet still divided by the page-laden table between them.

LAUGHING, SASHA AND CHAD fell backward onto the bed of another love hotel.

This was the third one today, and she was really racking up the bills with these look-sees for her research.

But, oh, was she getting great material.

"I never thought I'd see a place like this," she said. "I might not have even tried it before now. I think this trip has done something to me."

"Like what?"

Her first instinct was to smile secretively, but she wanted to put that behind her.

"I think," she said, "I'm ready to try everything."

After a pause, during which she caught Chad holding back an ecstatic grin, she got to her elbows on the mattress, glancing around a room that resembled a strange imitation of *Star Wars:* the bed was like a spaceship, and since it had the capacity to vibrate, it could send the occupants to light-speed. There was a facsimile of a desert-planet bar in one corner, with booze and containers full of condoms, and in another was a space station, complete with toy laser blasters that did heaven-knew-what to a body.

When Sasha had suggested this tour at the beginning of their day, she'd thought Chad's glasses might just about steam up. But she'd made it clear that this was for research purposes only. No funny stuff.

Little did he know, though, that with every hotel they visited, the more she reconsidered.

"What I'd give," Sasha said, tucking her hands under her head, "to be able to see how a real Japanese couple acts in one of these rooms. Now, I'm not talking about being a voyeur," she elaborated as Chad leaned on his elbow and raised his eyebrows at her. "I mean that this culture requires that they use two different ways of presenting themselves—one way is private and one way is public. It'd be enlightening to see how those ways vary."

"Analytical to the end."

She smiled, knowing that was true. But she hesitated to tell him that, since last night, she'd started seeing the world in another way, too.

She'd perceived that first bar they'd visited as a soft blue haven, the rose at the doorway as a burst of brilliant red.

But maybe that's what happened when you started to trust again, she thought. When you started to hope.

"There's a word for the differences in how they act," she added, her voice light. "*Honne* and *tatemae*. *Honne* is a sincerely felt response. *Tatemae* is the socially required one."

"There'd be lots of *honne* in here, I suspect," Chad said.

Sasha gently slapped his arm, and he laughed, got up and figured out how to work the vibrating feature on the bed.

Sasha lay still, even when the wild lights on the ceiling began to flash to space music.

The cadence of them was hypnotic, making her eyelids heavy, especially since last night had gone late and they'd been doing nothing but running around today.

Thinking she might just close her eyes for a moment, she succumbed to the buzzing of the bed as Chad returned to lie beside her.

Even though they were in an odd place—the last place she would have ever pictured herself—she felt…

Sasha smiled. She felt comfortable, she supposed. But that might have been because Chad was here. She had spent so many nights remembering what it had been like that his presence seemed perfectly natural.

She must've even fallen asleep, because before she knew it, she was groggily opening her eyes again, finding herself reclining on her side with Chad cradling her.

The scent of him, the *feel* of him, was so familiar that she started to drift off again.

Until she realized that, just as in old times, his hand was covering her breast.

Her eyes widened, a shock of adrenaline shaking her.

Too soon, her mind shouted.

But, months ago, she'd woken up so many mornings with him in exactly this position that she didn't want to move.

God help her, she'd missed this, and as he drew in a long breath, stirring the stray hair at her nape, she pressed his hand closer to her.

A lump burned in her throat. She loved him so much. Had never stopped.

As his breathing hushed over the back of her neck, desire charred her—starting in her belly, pushing outward until it pained.

Chad.

If not now, when? When would she stop blaming him—and herself—for what hadn't worked the first time?

They'd learned from being apart, hadn't they? And she'd even learned something within these past few days—to be more willing to step out of her marked borders, to go for it.

So what was stopping her from taking those lessons and applying them to the biggest leap of faith she could take?

Her breathing trembled as she shifted, feeling his body,

long and lean, in back of her. His thighs, his groin, his torso, his arms that were still wrapped around her.

She'd wanted independence, but she wanted this, too.

Wanted him with all her heart.

Fingers clumsy, she tentatively undid the first button of her blouse, then continued on down until she could slip her hand inside to unhook the front of her bra.

Then she exhaled, her pulse choppy as she turned onto her back. Chad's hand slipped to her ribs and, with a bit less caution this time, she hauled the rest of her shirt and bra away from her chest.

She closed her eyes once more.

No going back if you do this, she thought.

It was time. Damned time.

Opening her eyes, she took his hand and placed it on her naked breast. A soft groan wracked her—a wildness clawing to get out that she had never really allowed free before.

So long, too long without him.

His breathing had gone from long and rhythmic to a quicker pace, and she guessed he'd woken up.

When he cupped her breast and whispered her name, that only confirmed it.

He'd taken off his glasses, leaving him free to bury his entire face against her neck, his lips still shaping her name, repeating it between the kisses he pressed on her.

Body shimmering with heat, she rolled over to face him, to crush her mouth to his in a kiss she'd been dreaming about for months.

But the musky taste of him, the way their lips and tongues attacked and slipped and slid, was real.

Acute and real.

She pressed her sex to his, feeling him rising against his pants. Riding a crash of need, she lifted her leg to drape it over his. She pushed against him, getting him harder.

"I love you," he said on a moan.

The words thundered into her, through her.

She'd always kept the confession back, taming it, but she let it out now.

"Me, too," she said, the admission scratching her throat but sounding so right and good. "I love you, too, Chad."

As he whisked off her blouse and bra entirely, then his own shirt, she reveled in the press of her breasts to his bare chest, her nipples hard against his hair-sprinkled skin. The peaks of her combed through that hair, sending keen screams of sensation through every cell of her body.

Her pants came next, then his, and soon they were fitted to each other, his erection prodding between her thighs.

She felt as if she were being split in two: the public side of her versus the sincerely felt. The fear versus the desire for love. The analytical Sasha against the one who really did want to see the world in bursts of colors.

"I'm on the way," he said in a harsh whisper.

And she could feel that, because his head was already slick with beaded moisture.

"We've got time," she answered. "As many times as we want."

She touched his penis, the length of it so natural in her hand.

Then she circled her thumb over his tip, stroking into the wet slit at the very top.

He groaned, long and tortured, and Sasha slid her other

hand down to his balls, where she knew the pleasure of touch would undo him.

Then she rolled him to moaning ecstasy.

But he had other plans.

"I want to be inside you for this," he said, sitting up and straddling her while pinning her arms over her head. "I've been waiting a long time, and I don't want to be on the outside when it happens, Sasha."

She didn't disagree with him, because the last place she wanted him ever to be again was on the outside.

He traveled one hand down, then over the sensitive crook of her underarm, and she jerked, her sex giving a startling pulse of need.

Then he came to her breast, taking her nipple between his fingers and working it.

She arched her hips, his penis skimming her belly. That split she'd felt earlier was stronger now, wedging her apart, thrusting her into the sincerely felt side.

When he bent to take her other nipple into his mouth, a stab of pleasure tore into her so strongly that she shot to a climax there and then.

Her core spasmed, but he kept on sucking, manipulating, bringing her higher, urging her to the precipice of another orgasm.

He knew just what to do. He'd been the only one who'd *ever* known.

Almost subtly, he used his free hand to part her legs, then slipped his arousal right into her, smoothly, as if he belonged there.

And he did, she thought as she churned her hips, taking him in. It was as if he'd never left.

She was skating on thin ice now, cold and hot warring within her, pushing and pulling.

A rupture rattled her as Chad thrust into her harder, faster, and she knew she couldn't hold together.

So she grabbed onto him, moving with him, her body coming apart inch by inch until—

—*CRACK*—

She came again so brutally that she cried out at the top of her lungs, digging her fingers into him.

As she was coming down, he was peaking, gushing into her, until he collapsed against her.

While they held each other, Sasha felt the separated side of her floating away as she clung to the other.

The *honne* side. The love.

The colors, she thought as she hugged Chad even tighter.

10

JULIANA AND TRISTAN merely looked at each other in the aftermath of reading.

They were both speechless, she thought, numbed, as if neither of them really knew how to proceed.

But maybe she was also still recovering from what he'd said to her beforehand, about how he'd wanted her to be with him when they were young instead of leaving him behind in solitude and secrecy. She'd always hoped he'd been wishing for that, and it ripped at her that neither of them had ever risked themselves to find out the truth.

That they had never taken the chance on the seed of what they'd had during those few summer nights.

Juliana finally spoke. "The journal pages—it's clear that Terrence loved Emelie more than I've ever been told."

"And she felt the same about him." Tristan tossed down the copies. "Everything that happened between them after they broke up was needless. All the fighting, all the time they wasted…"

He was pissed, but she suspected it was a mask for sadness, too, because that's what she was feeling.

Sadness for two people—and two families—who had truly misspent all these years being bitter.

Sadness for how things could've been mended so much earlier and how it would've allowed them to fall in love.

But had this really changed anything?

How did knowing the extent of Terrence and Emelie's love for each other alter the competition for the painting—the token of a personal battle that had gotten way out of control?

A knock sounded on Tristan's door, and Juliana knew it was the maid summoning them downstairs.

She busied herself by gathering Emelie's letters and stuffing them in her sash.

"Hey," Tristan said.

Don't look at him, she thought. *If you do, he's going to see right through you. He's going to know that you're afraid of crashing and burning, just like Emelie and Terrence did. He's going to know that you want more than anything to reach across the table to touch his hand, to connect to him, when you know you shouldn't.*

But she couldn't help it.

He was watching her with something she'd never seen from anyone else—an emotion that wasn't like the comfort from an aunt or the warmth of a good friend, although it had those qualities somewhere underneath the intensity.

No, this was a look that shook her with a deep, desperate longing.

He came over to her, and her belly quivered. Just having him near undid her, and she came *this* close to telling him that he could just have the painting, that she would endure the consequences of a hurt, betrayed family for him.

Then the reality of what that would feel like—the injured looks, the disbelief that she'd turned against them—smacked into Juliana.

She'd put her life on hold, sold her business, to aid and support her family. And even though a part of her resented that, a part of her had really wanted to do it, too, because you didn't just desert the ones who'd dropped everything for you after your parents had died, when you'd needed help the most.

It was this part that won out now.

She took his hand in hers, the quavers in her tummy spiraling into whirls of heat. Her body seemed to fold into itself, pressing against her heart.

"I wish things could be different," she said.

His hand fell out of hers. "I wish you saw that they could be."

Averting his face, he left her, heading for the door as she fought the sharpness in her throat and chest. His blocked expression didn't hide the slump of his otherwise strong shoulders.

But he wasn't looking at everything realistically, she thought, her lungs feeling squeezed. He'd let the fairy-tale portion of Terrence and Emelie's letters sway him and was ignoring all the tangles that had come afterward.

The maid led them downstairs, to a larger room that held a big, dark, square lacquered table that hovered over the *tatami*.

Jiro Mori and a *yukata*-wearing woman with a pleasant smile and short, bobbed hair were waiting for them. In the corner, Juliana also saw a covered easel through the blur of barely checked tears, and she knew that the painting was beneath the sheet.

Her heart twisted. *Dream Rising.*

The reason for all the pain.

But she called on her deepest strength to do business, engaging in greetings all around, pushing back those tears. Jiro introduced his female associate as Midori Sakai, who was here to authenticate *Dream Rising.* Then he motioned for Juliana and Tristan to sit in their floor-bound chairs while maids brought them tea.

Jiro and Midori walked to the painting, as if eager to unveil it.

"It's quite a work," the woman said in perfect, British-inflected English.

Juliana found herself glancing at Tristan, who looked back at her with eyes that had darkened to a troubled gray. She wished she could know what he was thinking without having to take the scary chance of responding to whatever he might put out there.

Best not say a word. Best get this painting business behind them so they could go home and...

Her chest felt as if it were caving in again.

Jiro's voice jammed its way between her and Tristan's shared gaze, and broke the link, leaving her with a hollow feeling that she couldn't identify.

"Are you ready to see it?" the art dealer asked.

"Yes," Juliana said too quickly.

Out of her peripheral vision, she could see Tristan give a slight nod, as if he wasn't entirely focused on the art, either.

Jiro turned to his associate. "Midori-san?"

Carefully, the woman uncovered the painting, and a hush fell over the room as the rain on the roof faded into the background.

The colors, was the first thing Juliana thought, her hand coming up to her throat. She hadn't expected the intensity of crimson at the bottom of the painting, hadn't known she'd be so moved by how it turned into a violet mist as Emelie's slim arms reached up and outward.

Juliana had expected Terrence to use a canvas of his usual blues, but this was a bleeding, naked admission of passion from Terrence's brush, and it prodded Juliana's heart, made her throat ache all over again.

Love. She had never seen such a joyous yet heartbreaking expression of it, and she wasn't sure she could even have identified it before now.

She glanced down before she gave away the extremes of her agony. She didn't know a thing about falling for someone so hard that you perceived the world in arresting hues.

Or did she?

Midori had launched into an explanation of how she knew the painting was the real thing, citing something about how Terrence Cole always included his initials in an intricate winding of letters near the bottom of his watercolors.

When she finished, Jiro watched Juliana and Tristan expectantly, but neither of them said anything.

There was silence until she heard herself talking about what she'd read in Terrence's journal.

"So tragic," she said, her voice sounding as if it were caught up in the mist of the painting itself. She wasn't even sure who she was talking to—Tristan, Jiro…or herself. "I knew Emelie loved Terrence and had been hurt by his rejection, but now I know he was in anguish about letting her go, too." Her throat rubbed against every word. "He hated that they had no future, hated that his family already had his bride chosen for him. He didn't want to part with Emelie, but he was loyal to his family, and he tried to show her how much she meant to him with this painting. He intended always to keep it with him, thinking he could at least hold that much of her, that no one could ever take it away." She swallowed. "But Emelie needed—*wanted*—more than that. She wanted all of him, and she should have had it. They just never got it together, Terrence and Emelie."

She could feel Tristan watching her again.

It was all she *could* feel, really.

Her hand slid away from her throat, dropping to her lap. "He painted what he saw in her," she added, talking to Tristan now. Only Tristan. "But at the same time, this watercolor was *his* soul, too. Emelie was his soul. And it's no wonder your family never made Terrence's journal public. It showed too much of him. It showed..." *Don't say it.*

But she did.

"It showed all his hopes for what he and Emelie could have had together."

Tristan's voice eased into the gaping pause that hers had left. "They could still have it."

His tone—low and emotional—rocked her.

She didn't look at him. To do so would break her down, and she couldn't have that.

As if they'd forgotten anybody else was in the room, Tristan continued.

"The way she saw it," he said, "Terrence had meant the work to go to her. It was all she had left of him, too, and having it was the only thing that kept her together after she had to turn away. That painting kept her strong for the few days she had it before it was genuinely stolen. But she'd already sketched it in that letter to her sister." Tristan was still watching Juliana. "Memories of it bolstered her through the roughest times, but she—they—could've had so much more if he'd gone against his family and refused the arranged engagement."

Don't look at him, Juliana reminded herself.

She forced her gaze to the painting, and in it, she saw those reaching hands, the desperate stretch of them.

But instead of seeing Emelie, she saw a woman who'd lost love because she didn't know how to handle it.

Everything came to Juliana in a rush, as if the mist were enveloping her: having sex with Tristan, rising, rising toward the height of her feelings, then having to pull back from all its strength because giving all of herself to him was a betrayal.

How could she shake that?

Would she ever be able to?

She heard someone clear his throat, then realized it was Jiro.

"So then," their host said, the pep in his voice indicating that he knew just how much *Dream Rising* had cost their families...and would cost one of them now. "I believe we're prepared to continue."

Continue.

He made it sound so easy.

But couldn't it be?

As she stole a last glance at Tristan while the negotiations began, she let herself wonder.

AFTER THE BARGAINING ended, Jiro provided them with an exquisite multicourse dinner that was a work of art in itself, composed of everything from sashimi to beef-wrapped asparagus to tempura shrimp to fresh fruit for dessert.

Tristan expressed his enjoyment of it, of course, although his stomach had churned the whole time. Even after he'd holed up in his room, post-meal, to call Chad, he felt immune to sensation.

When his cousin answered, he sounded sleepy-voiced, content....

Tristan didn't ask.

Instead, he said, "Two hundred and fifty thousand American dollars. Can you get the cash in motion?"

He could hear the immediate change in Chad's tone. "You did it? You beat the Thomsens out for the painting?"

"I did it."

His voice was flat, but how could it be anything else next to the words of Terrence and Emelie? Or against the image of *Dream Rising,* with its colors and shapes weaving into a message that had entered Tristan, making him see what he and Juliana truly had with each other?

Love—or at least the concept of it. It was complicated, hard to bottle, but it possessed him all the same.

His glance rested on a dripping branch in the garden. He would swear that she was just as in love with him as he was with her. They were meant to be. They always had been.

Chad was talking. "Over two hundred thousand. That's a steep price to pay."

He had no idea just how much Tristan had invested. "But the family's got it covered. It'll stretch the bank accounts, but the money's there."

"True."

He could tell Chad wanted to talk longer, but Tristan signed off, then shoved his phone into his bag.

He wasn't about to leave the *ryokan* without seeing her again, without...

There was a tap at his door.

Thinking it was the maid, he called for her to enter.

It wasn't the maid, and his electrified body, his thudding pulse confirmed it.

Long, light hair spilling over her face, hiding her expression from him, Juliana doffed her slippers, then came all the way into his room, tucking the strands behind her ears.

So sad, he thought. But weren't they both?

"Congratulations," she said. "It wouldn't be polite to go home without saying it here first."

"You already did say it, after we closed our business and again during the meal with Jiro and Midori."

He wanted to ask her why she was here—to make her say it—but he didn't want to scare her off.

But he'd get her to admit it before she left this room. Dammit, he wouldn't go back to the States without her.

Juliana stepped closer, and a fan in the corner blew enough air to lift the ends of her hair. He imagined the feel of its softness against his face.

"Did you tell them yet?" he asked.

"I called, but my uncle Gary answered." Juliana pressed her lips together, then barely got the words out. "Aunt Katrina was so anxious about the negotiations that they put her to bed."

"You're kidding—"

"No, she's okay, but she gets like this sometimes. I'm

afraid one day that her 'nerve flutters' will turn into something worse, so I'm dreading how she'll react when she actually hears about the painting."

The rest went unsaid: how Aunt Katrina might respond if she also found out about her great-niece and Tristan.

It enraged him that the family could manipulate Juliana like this. The whole town knew how sweet yet controlling Katrina Thomsen could be.

He stood, came toward her. "Juliana."

Next thing he knew, she was against him, her face pressed against his chest, her arms around his waist. He was so surprised that he paused, then tenderly stroked a hand down her hair, holding her to him.

Oh, God. This couldn't end. It just couldn't.

"I can't test her," she said. "It would be selfish of me."

"I've thought the same thing. But doesn't there come a point where they should think about our happiness? Why does an abstract feud count more, Juliana?"

He cupped her face, guided her to look at him. The tears in her eyes almost killed him.

He couldn't stand to see her like this, and he knew that, if they went back home and announced their relationship to the town, there'd be a lot more tears.

Maybe for the rest of their lives.

She pressed her cheek back to him, and all he could do was hold her.

And afterward?

He just didn't know anymore.

JULIANA DIDN'T WANT to let go of him.

Never.

But she had the sinking feeling that if she made a choice here, it would be much harder to keep back in Parisville, where consequences would rush back to greet her with battering speed.

So would this be the last time she saw Tristan?

Would they be like Terrence and Emelie, living in the same town but separated by a refusal to give in to their hearts?

All she knew was that she was here with Tristan now, and they still had the night.

Then it'd be homeward bound. Real life.

No more playtime in Wonderland.

Against her, he felt hard, strong, and she got even closer to him, feeling safe and warm now.

One more time, she thought. One last memory to make.

He must've been thinking the same thing, because he inched his hands between them to part her robe.

Then his robe.

Their bare skin touched, burned, and she gasped, feeling his penis rubbing against her belly. He was getting aroused, his tip probing her, already wet.

Without breaking contact, she bent one leg, then the other, slipping off her socks.

Then she doffed her robe while he did the same with his.

Her blood dove downward to pool and whirl, to harden her clit until she wanted to touch it and soothe the gnawing stiffness.

She ran her hands over his toned waist, his rear.

She wanted to paint him, just like Terrence and Emelie's picture, show him how much he meant. That way, maybe he'd always be able to feel it, to see that maybe they could find a way to be together someday.

He got to one knee, spreading his *yukata* on the ground as an impromptu bed. The maid would be laying out a futon later, so this would have to do for now.

Anything would do.

The intensity of his gray gaze brought her to her knees and they kneeled face-to-face, him holding her hands in his.

It seemed to be a promise that they would overcome everything, but she couldn't believe that. She wanted to, but she knew her fiction and the line between that and fact.

At some point, she'd become a realist, and that fact hurt just as much as loving Tristan did.

And she did love him. Maybe she always had.

HE SAW THE DESPERATION in her gaze, and when she slid her hand underneath his penis, the shock of contact fried him.

Did he *want* it fast and desperate with her?

His body said an unqualified yes, but his heart said no. It wanted slow and lasting.

It wanted everything she wasn't able to give right now.

"Juli—" he started to say.

Her name snagged in his throat as she ran her cupped palm upward, then down.

Breath. Heart. Both had stopped....

"I want to make you happy," she said, using her other hand to urge him to his back. "Let me make you as happy as I can right now, Tristan."

As he reclined, she touched her own sex, and when

she brought her fingers out, she smoothed that hand over his cock, stroking up and down, coating him with her juices.

Just knowing that she'd already been so worked up for him shot a jolt through his body—thousands of watts.

Why couldn't it be this way in the future, too?

All his possible answers shorted out when she held the base of him with one hand, her knuckles facing her, her thumb resting on his pubic hair. Then she smoothed upward, grasping him gently until she got to his head, where she made a twisting motion, sliding her palm over his other side while continuing to grasp him on the way down, her knuckles facing him now.

When she got to the base of him again, her other hand took the place of the first and soon she established one continuous, sinuous rhythm with both hands.

It felt as if liquid were running over him—hard liquid—and he dropped all the way to his back, unable to do anything more than feel an orgasm building.

He tried to say her name once more, maybe to stop her because she was hitting every sensitive inch of him, killing him with each twisting caress at his tip.

Or maybe he was only trying to tell her what she did to him—not just to his body, but to everything else, to the part of him that had stayed remote from all the others because Juliana and only Juliana had been his ideal.

"Show me you're happy," Juliana said. "Let me remember it."

With every twist of her wrist as she came to his tip, he saw how much she needed him to show her.

She increased the pressure and pace, and he grabbed

at the robe under him, pulling on it, fighting the heat steaming inside him.

The red mist in the painting...

The way it hissed and lifted and—

He spilled his juices in bursts, bathing his belly, her hands, and when he was done, Juliana still held him, sketching his head with her thumb.

He saw the emotion buried beneath the violet of her eyes, a color as soft as dusk, just before the sun disappeared.

If it wasn't love, he'd be wrong the rest of his life. She felt the same way he felt about her. He knew it.

Rage speared him—anger at the world, at what was ruining their chance to be together.

Sitting up, he grabbed her by the waist and tugged her to him. Her sex rested against his cock, and he almost lost all train of thought at the slippery warmth of her.

She held him tightly, and he trailed his fingers downward, over her cheek, her neck, to her chest.

He pressed against her heart.

"I want to believe it's enough that I'll be in here," he said. "But it's not, Juliana. It'll never be enough."

"Tristan..."

She was racked with guilt, he thought. Just as out-of-mind wary as he was about going *there*.

"Juliana," he said again, but this time all his emotions were entwined with her name.

In her gaze, he saw her vacillate, saw her flail and wonder what to do.

He leaned forward, kissed her just over her breast, where her heart beat like something trying to escape from its hiding place.

Her hands tightened on his shoulders, and he dragged his mouth to her nipple, taking it into his mouth to circle his tongue around, to taste her sweat, to suck and kiss.

She whimpered, and he slipped his fingers over her belly, to her legs, opened them and ran a soft touch over her inner thighs.

She jerked, winced, and he continued, petting her there, up and down her damp skin, coming closer and closer to her pussy.

At the same time, he kept sucking, working her nipple while slowly easing her back to the ground.

Then he switched his mouth to her other breast, still caressing between her legs as she wiggled her hips, insisting that he go on.

He let go of her breast, wanting to see her face.

And when he spied her flushed skin—a lightly brush-stroked rose—he went hard again.

"Every night," he whispered. "We could have this every night, Juliana…"

At the sound of his voice, she opened her eyes, as if realizing what was happening.

But in the next moment, she closed them again, tightly, turning her head away as she began to moan.

He increased the pace of his stroking, and she moaned again, louder.

Then again.

Again…

She was fighting it, he thought.

But he was going to get her over it.

11

EVEN THOUGH HER SKIN was on fire, her body pulsing into itself, the enormity of being here with him kept coming back to Juliana.

Don't think about anything but Tristan, she told herself, shifting her hips in response to his caresses. Moving with him.

Don't think about them.

His fingers rested on her inner thighs, brushing close to the center of her, and she ached. Agonized.

"I'm not going to give up," Tristan murmured as he sketched his palm up to her mons.

She bit her lip, hard. It felt as if a part of herself—an entirely new part—was breaking away from her, away from her regular loyalties.

Can't let go, she thought, every worst-case scenario running through her mind. Being left alone, just as she'd almost been when she was little, without her parents, until the family had come to claim her....

Tristan bent to place a soft kiss on her breast. Then he sent her a glance of such affection that a warm gush flooded her veins.

"Wouldn't it be worth every second of misery?" he asked.

Yes, she thought. *It would.*

Then he kissed her again, under the curve of her breast this time, and when his lips left her skin she pressed toward him, arcing her back, hating to lose contact.

No one had ever been so patient with her...or so persistent. No other man had been so willing to invest this much effort and care.

The realization screwed into her belly, digging down until her clit stiffened to a painful piercing. Then the sensation flamed upward, taking her to where she'd started.

The zing of need wedged her open as he ground a thumb against her clit, then took her nipple into his mouth again—but harder this time, the wet, wicked suction so unbearable that she almost screamed.

He drew on her. "Beautiful Juliana," he whispered. "Perfect Juliana."

Echoes from the past, when he'd said the same words to her in the car one time, holding her close, kissing her neck in innocent fervor, melded with the present.

I never stopped needing him, she thought. *I won't ever stop.*

She almost sobbed at the thought of it, but it was true, and the idea helped her shed the guilt she'd been feeling, leaving her to thread her fingers through his hair, holding on to him.

Yes, Juliana would go back home to her family, but she would always love him.

The thought freed her, making her ten times more open. Sensitive...

He moved to her other breast, his every motion slow and worshipful, as if he would take forever with her. She tightened her hold as he nipped at her peak, licking it to an even more stimulated nub. His tongue took up the same rhythm as the fingers stroking her sex.

Juliana moaned as if in anguish—drunken, delightful pain that was making her feel more animated than ever.

And when he slid his fingers into her, slipping his thumb over her clit while still loving her breast with his tongue, Juliana's moan turned to a blissed-out mewl.

She spread her legs for him, inviting him deeper inside.

He looked just as flushed and excited as she was, and lowered her to the ground, taking hold of his erection with one hand, then guiding it between her legs. The tip of him slicked against her, and she instinctively raised her hips.

"Now," she said, unable to wait another pulse-thrashing second.

He plunged inside with one thrust.

As she took him, she cried out his name because he filled her. And as he drove into her once more, another time, he broke her apart, pounding into her, then beating her back together again.

A rumble growled inside Juliana, growing in sound and fury.

They looked into each other's eyes as they labored, as she pushed against the ground with one hand as if that could bring her even closer to him—maybe even *into* him.

He really was a part of her now, and she couldn't deny it.

The rumble in her core opened into a full-fledged quake, and the split cracked farther up her body as tiny fissures jabbed out from her center, outward, upward, increasing in speed, breaking into their own multitude of fault lines.

Then there was something like a gush, a thundering wall of water rushing through the cracks of her, blasting her apart until only scatters of thought could form before being obliterated, too.

Him.

Her Tristan...

She was still coming when he climaxed, as if her orgasm had been the thing that had broken him, as well.

The force continued to pummel at her, disintegrating her...

Section by section...

One piece...

Another...

Then, following what seemed like hours, she spasmed one last time, pulling him down to her, burying her face in his neck, almost biting him with the aftershocks.

His skin tasted of salt, sweat and musk, and it got her even drunker as their chests rose and fell together, trying to find a compatible cadence. Her nipples were tender and raw against him, and nothing had ever felt better.

She struggled for air, holding him tighter as a tremor buzzed her belly, then her limbs.

As their breathing leveled, she kept holding him, knowing it was almost time to let go.

But the more she clung, the flimsier her reasons for leaving him behind seemed.

That would wear off, she thought, calling upon the practicality that had gotten her through school, through the heartache of giving up her business and freedom, to go back to Parisville.

It would have to wear off, or she'd go insane.

His mouth moved to a tender spot below her ear, and she hoped he didn't think that one last fling had changed her mind.

She closed her eyes, hating herself, but knowing she'd feel the same way if she chose him over her family, too.

Powerless, she thought. Love shouldn't leave her this way.

As if sensing the train of her thoughts, Tristan's muscles tensed and in the endless heartbeat of their silence, the rebel in Juliana goaded her to imagine what it might be like to finally come out to her family—to stand up for who she was and what she might want if she could only have it.

But even after the mantra of saying goodbye to Girl Friday she'd infused herself with on this trip, she'd only been kidding herself.

"So this is it," he said against her skin.

She spoke into his hair, holding him tighter. "This has to be it."

As he hugged her to him, she told herself that they were doing the right thing.

Even if it left her empty inside.

"JULIANA, DO YOU HAVE the hammer and nails?" Sasha asked, walking into the box-strewn living room of her apartment two weeks later. Even though she was dressed in sweats, she managed to look as put together as ever. A brisk ocean breeze floated through the open window and wisped the hair curling down to her shoulders.

But maybe the togetherness was due to the smile that never seemed to leave Sasha's face now that she'd decided to move just a half hour away from Parisville, to a town near the Pacific coast.

Juliana, who was sitting on the red faux-leather sofa, raised the hammer to her friend. "Here it is, Sash."

"Perfect."

The other woman was carrying a cityscape-inspired watercolor that she'd found in a Tokyo flea market and had had shipped home.

After Juliana had returned to the States, Sasha and Chad had stayed an extra week, doing more research for her book by staying in their own *ryokan* and taking moonlight walks during which they'd discovered more exotic surprises. They'd be going back soon for a much longer trip, after Sasha got settled.

She climbed on the sofa barefoot and positioned the painting this way and that on the wall. "So what do you think? Is it a good centerpiece for the room or should I go with something more Elvis on velvet?"

"Either or." Juliana barely even glanced at the painting. She never wanted to see a watercolor again.

Her friend caught her absentmindedness right away, lowering herself and the painting back to the sofa to give Juliana her full attention.

"You've become the mopiest moper who ever moped, and I have no idea how to snap you out of it." Nonetheless, Sasha snapped her fingers in front of Juliana's face, as if that would perform a miracle.

Juliana hated being a moper, so she did her best to perk up. But she knew it was just her latest façade.

Hadn't she decided to drop it?

But that was hard, knowing Tristan had been back

home for a while, also. Besides, her family wasn't exactly in the best of moods, and going to work most days with a good deal of the Thomsen clan was like treading through a bog.

Sasha sighed. "If you and the rest of the family are this bummed out now, I'd hate to see you guys in an hour."

"Oh, believe me, there'll be nothing but fireworks then." The Coles were throwing a big shindig at the community center by the town square, where *Dream Rising* would be the guest of honor.

Her family was taking great exception to the Coles' gloating, and there was bound to be some trouble in Parisville. Juliana had heard the older crowd whispering, and she just knew they would do something mortifying like crashing the party or at least hanging around near it to show that they could still face the Coles.

She wondered if Tristan would be there, if, maybe, they could look at each other across the chaos and laugh, knowing they were above this.

But if that were true, wouldn't she have the guts to be with him?

Dammit, she wished she did have the guts, because living without him wasn't working. She couldn't stop thinking about him, feeling him against her, sinking into near depression when she told herself that he would never be touching her again. She missed the way he laughed, missed how adventurous she felt when she was with him.

Sasha rested her painting against the side of the couch. "And here I thought Japan had... I don't know. Changed things."

"For you."

"And you." Sasha's gaze was no-nonsense. "But I guess you were just all talk about freedom and exploration."

Juliana jerked at that because it was true. After feeling so different on the trip, she'd come back to the same old life, the same old thing that she'd been so intent on escaping.

And she was already sick of it. Hell, she'd been sick of it the first day back, when she'd been met at the airport with good-try-but-no-cigar disappointment by her aunt and five cousins. They hadn't blamed her for missing out on *Dream Rising* exactly, but the reminder of her failure had been there just the same.

She'd wanted to shout at them: "There's so much more in the world than this small-minded crap!" But how could she say that when she didn't have the courage to break out of the Thomsen mold fully herself?

Sasha had placed her hand on Juliana's arm, as if to soften her comment, but it still rang through her.

That's when Chad wandered in, comfortable in old blue jeans, a Coldplay T-shirt and his glasses. His sandy hair was ruffled, but he didn't seem to care.

"Erm…" he said, "I couldn't help overhearing from the other room…"

Sasha got up from the couch and sidled up to him, tapping his chest in mock chastisement.

"Spying on the enemy camp?" she asked.

They both laughed. These days, Chad had better things to invest himself in than a family feud.

"Listen," he said, talking to Juliana, "if it makes you feel any better, since Tristan got back, he hasn't come out of either his personal garage or the business one in town.

He even cut his own Japan trip short, sticking around just long enough to meet with his vintage-car client."

The news didn't make her feel any better. She hated that Tristan had gone back to his old ways, too.

Sasha hugged Chad, causing Juliana's heart to ache.

"If you've been listening closely, Jules," her friend said as she rested her head against Chad's shoulder. "My man here was trying to tell you that Tristan's just as destroyed as your sad self. He's head over heels for you, and you're the same way for him. If love isn't worth fighting for, what is?"

She didn't tell them that she asked herself this over and over, arguing that she'd chosen love of her family.

But Sasha was right: how often did love come around?

Wasn't it worth seeing if it was time for a change with *everyone?*

Her heart kicked at her chest, and Juliana put her hand there to calm herself.

What if Emelie and Terrence had swallowed their pride and run to each other—him not expecting her to settle for being a secret mistress and her not faulting him for considering the arranged marriage?

What if they had confronted his family and told them that they had no option but to work with it?

Sasha's voice urged Juliana on. "Jules...?"

Juliana glanced up to see both Sasha and Chad watching her, as if all they wanted was for her to get the hope permanently back into her own gaze.

She remembered wanting the same for Sasha once upon a time.

Don't let history repeat itself, she thought.

"Is Tristan planning to come out of his garage today?"

Juliana asked. "Or do I have to hunt him down like we did that painting?"

Sasha and Chad broke into huge smiles as Juliana's pulse broke free.

A WASTED SATURDAY, Tristan thought as he lounged on a metal chair in the corner of the community center, buried behind the throng of jubilant Coles who'd come from near and far to party in Parisville.

There was wine and beer in raised glasses, the aroma of buffalo wings and other party grub lacing the air, cheery social voices. There were even streamers draped from the ceiling, and above it all, on the dais, *Dream Rising* reigned.

His relatives kept toasting him, and he kept doing it back, his heart hardly in it.

Not when he missed her so much.

Juliana.

The brightness of her hair, the color of her eyes… Everything else seemed drab in comparison.

Strange, he thought, how they'd found each other all the way over in Japan, and yet here in this small town, they were farther apart than ever.

His mother, who had wound her black hair, burgeoning with glints of silver, in a bun, smiled at him as she brought Gramps over in his wheelchair. The old man had always favored his daughter-in-law above all the others, and after Tristan's dad had died, the two had become closer than ever, with her acting as his nurse.

The old man, his shriveled legs bent together as if they were two thin branches leaning on each other for support, beamed at his grandson.

"Tristan," he said. "The man of the hour."

Tristan's heart swelled at the joy in his grandfather's bright eyes, but it was short-lived when he realized that the happiness was only based on a damned picture.

He only wished Terrence and Emelie could be here to tell everyone that this was nothing to celebrate at all.

His mom seemed to know something was amiss with him—it was there in her gray eyes. Maybe she recognized a broken heart so well because she'd been carrying one around with her ever since his dad had passed on.

"Join the party," she said. "We've missed you."

Miss, he thought. Nobody here but her probably understood the meaning of that as well as he did.

"I'll just keep taking things in over here, if it's all the same," he said.

"Now, now," Gramps said. "The hero shouldn't be put in a corner."

As his mom turned his grandfather around in his chair, she gave Tristan a sympathetic glance, and he smiled to assure her that nothing was wrong.

Nothing except everything.

The party went on, and under the smooth stereo voice of Frank Sinatra, Tristan noticed that Chad and Sasha had arrived and were trapped near the door by some New York cousins.

Soon afterward, the chatting and carousing came to an abrupt stop.

Then someone turned off the music.

Tristan stood, spying the cause of the disturbance right away.

Thomsens.

A group of them had wandered into the community center, just as casual as could be, holding their own wine bottles and waving at everyone as if they'd been invited.

Juliana? he thought, starting forward, thinking she might be with them, before he told himself to stop.

Tristan sank back onto his chair. Of course she wasn't here, and it was pathetic that he could barely bring himself to move without her around.

Shit. He should've done something two weeks ago—should've gone with his gut and told her that she did things to him that he'd never experienced with a woman before; she made the world come alive, made him want to see more of it rather than keeping himself under the dimness of a car.

Yet he'd gone and accepted the alternative once again, just like a whipped boy who didn't have a brave bone in his body.

Why?

Why accept it, when that's what had gotten Terrence and Emelie into such trouble?

Out of the corner of his eye, Tristan saw that his mom was wheeling his grandfather onto the stage in reaction to the Thomsens.

She halted his chair at the foot of *Dream Rising*.

Naturally, Tristan thought. Gramps wouldn't kick out the Thomsens. He'd do everything he could to revel in the painting—the Coles' victory.

A murmur came from the crowd, a tense undertow from both families.

Then he heard it—the voice floating through his memories during every waking hour.

"It just goes on and on, doesn't it?"

Was he...? Had he just heard...?

His heartbeat suspended.

He turned around, and the sight of her—the punch of her violet eyes—almost took him down.

Speechless. Frozen with such emotion he could hardly contain it.

"And," Juliana added, "it might just keep going on, with or without us."

She didn't have to say the rest.

I'm standing up for what I want now, and it's you.

Overcome, he took her in his arms, lifting her and plastering her body to his as his pulse zoomed once again.

And, in front of everyone, Tristan Cole kissed Juliana Thomsen, just as he'd wanted to do over fourteen years ago.

12

As Tristan's mouth crushed Juliana's, she spun down a rabbit hole, dizzy and full of bursting sensations.

They were finally claiming each other, no matter the consequences, and with every moment, the shadows stripped away from her as she fell down and down to where a light gaped at the end of the hole.

And she plunged into it headfirst.

Out of breath, she came up for air, but she still kept her lips against his as they both smiled, giddy.

"So this is it?" he asked, an echo of that day they'd said goodbye in the *ryokan*.

She laughed, kissed him again.

Someone in the back of the room shouted, but she didn't know what they said. Then someone else at the front of the room called out.

While kissing the man she was meant for, she'd almost forgotten the feud.

As she and Tristan turned their heads to the rising rumble, keeping their cheeks against each other's, Juliana's vision cleared enough to see fingers pointing at them. Even Tristan's grandfather, who was still on the stage, was trying to get out of his chair in his effort to make sure his own voice was heard above the rest.

But, next to him, Tristan's mom was smiling.

At that point, everything went into motion as the yells unmuddled themselves in Juliana's brain, turning into actual words:

"Tristan, you dumbass."

"Juliana, what the hell are you *doing?*"

Then she saw Chad and Sasha making their way through the crowd, playing peacemakers.

While the voices erupted around them, Tristan let Juliana slide down the front of his body, where she felt every last muscular inch of him against her.

Home, she thought.

"Consequence time," he said to her over the noise.

"How about we get the hell out of here?" she said, inclining her head toward the nearest exit.

His smile just about took her out at the knees as he grabbed her hand.

They parted the crowd, ignoring every question on their way to the door. It took only a few seconds to get out of the cacophony and into his gleaming red pickup.

As a few curious partygoers followed them into the parking lot, Tristan burned rubber out of there.

Head tilted back in laughter—genuine, cleansing and so right—Juliana didn't ask where they were going.

She didn't care, as long as she was with him.

Only a mile down the road her mirth gave way to the same nerves that had been twanging at her, just before she'd entered the community center with the rest of her clan to seek out Tristan among the crowd.

He was quiet, too.

She held to the edge of her seat. "I wouldn't be surprised if our families showed up on both of our doorsteps within the hour."

"Let them."

He sounded so cocksure about being able to handle anything that she absorbed his confidence.

This man did that for her, she thought. He made her want to be her own person for the first time in her life because she felt sure that he'd be worth the risk.

They were heading for the Cole ranch, down a dirt road lined with shading oaks, pristine white fences framing horses that meandered over the grass, then they turned into a stretching driveway.

Soon they arrived at a rustic cabin with a detached garage on the side and a wooden glider squatting on the porch. Straightforward and stalwart.

Tristan's place.

Once again, anxiety skipped over Juliana, because this cabin was *him*. She would be entering his private domain—not a hotel room or somewhere that was merely convenient for a few hours of fun—and it seemed like the hugest step she'd ever taken anywhere.

He got out of the truck, came around to her side, then opened the door for her.

As he stood there, with the warm inland wind tousling his dark hair, Juliana's limbs went light. He made her feel weak, but a good kind of weak.

He held out his hand to her, just as he'd done that day in front of the love hotel, inviting her over a different, even scarier threshold.

But this time, when she inhaled as she took hold of him, it wasn't because she was going against her family.

It was because she knew he would leave her breathless and she was preparing herself.

And—boom!—his fingers really did send shock waves through her as he helped her out of the truck, catching her and swinging her around, then bringing her up against his broad chest.

She buried her face in his neck, inhaling the scent of him—bay leaves, earthy, heady…

Oh, man.

Holding her, he walked her to his cabin, carrying her up the stairs as if she weighed close to nothing.

When they got to his door, he stopped, and she noticed how their hearts tagged each other beat by beat through their chests.

He was inside her again, she thought. Just in a different way now. A way that had nothing to do with sex.

Tristan used his fingers to push the hair back from her face, and the way he looked at her melted her from head to toe.

Then he opened his door, letting Juliana in and setting her on her feet.

The cabin's main room was as masculine as he was: shutters instead of curtains, flannel blankets tossed over the back of a pine futon, fishing gear in one corner and parts of an engine strewn over a table in another.

The personal details brought back something she'd said just before they'd left Japan—that even though they'd been intimate, she still didn't know much about him at all.

She wandered over to a window that enclosed a view of the sun-washed mountains in the near distance.

Heck, she didn't know why she'd gone across the room

when she could be in his arms. It'd been so easy to go to him in the community center.

But now?

Now came the hard part. The reality.

Just say something, she told herself.

"I don't have this sort of grand view at my apartment." Juliana didn't live on the main Thomsen property, with its batch of cottages. No, her place was a stucco-and-wood two-story box. It was close enough to the others that her family often dropped by, but far enough to maintain an illusion of space.

"It's something to wake up to every morning," he said, sounding just as awkward as she felt now that they'd made their stand.

Because what would come next? Would all their fears be realized about their families?

"Do you work out of this garage on your property, too?" she asked, motioning toward the building to the side of this one. Babbling. She was *so* babbling. "Or do you do your heavy work in your business garage in town?"

"I keep my pet projects here. Vintage finds. Things I don't want anyone else to get their hands on."

This. Was. Maddening.

And getting them nowhere.

She braced herself, turned her face away from the view, but didn't quite look at him yet. "You can ask it if you want to, Tristan."

"Ask what?"

Nerves. "How I came to change my mind and rescue you from that party."

He chuckled, and the sound winged over her skin.

"I hadn't even wondered," he said. "The second I saw you, I couldn't think of anything else."

She was going to melt away to nothing here.

Finally, Juliana turned all the way around to find him leaning against the wall, a small, content smile on his mouth. It was as if he were taking in the fact that she was here in his cabin, of all places, and he was just glad she'd finally made it.

A thrill spun around her chest. She was glad she'd made it, too.

"I knew my family was up to something," she said. "When I verified they were planning to crash the Cole celebration, I decided to make the most of it. I tagged along, except not for the reason they expected."

"And what made you do it, Juliana?"

She paused, her throat getting that searing, croaky feel to it. But she spoke around the ache.

"'As you get older,'" she said, "'you'll discover that the only things you regret are the things you didn't do.'"

He lifted his brows and his smile stretched even wider, as if he'd never met a woman who could quote—or at least paraphrase—Mark Twain right back at him.

"I missed the hell out of you," she added. "Couldn't sleep well. Couldn't eat much." She swallowed, and it burned. "There's no way I could go back to the way life was before. I'd tried it once, and I couldn't fake my way through the regret again."

At her confession, he gravitated toward her, and her pulse fluttered.

"If you hadn't shown up at the community center," he said, "I would've caught up to you somewhere else."

Unable to stand another minute across the room from him, she moved away from the window.

They met in the middle, where she could feel the heat coming off his flesh, could see pale flecks in his gray eyes.

Her heartbeat stomped in her temples, echoing in her chest. He excited her, and not just physically. Life became a dance of possibilities when he was around.

Her feelings for him were so intense that she laughed a bit, uncertain of how to react under these new rules.

"You ever get the feeling," she said, "that we did this in weird order?"

"First the puppy love, then the love hotel, then the love itself?"

The last word shot through the atmosphere, rattling into her.

Love.

She looked deeper into his eyes. It had only grown over time, from a fantasy into something they could both accept into their lives, shaping it in any way they wanted to.

He stroked her cheek, and she leaned into his caress.

Unable to resist a last tease, she gestured toward his fishing stuff in the corner. "Just so you know, I don't like getting up at ungodly hours to dangle hooks in a lake."

"So we'll pursue different hobbies. It'll make for great evening conversation on the porch at sunset."

"And I can't even tell you the difference between a Ford and a Dodge."

"Then I'll teach you if you want to know."

She smiled, but now it had nothing to do with teasing him. "I suspect there's a lot we could teach each other."

"I'm always a willing student."

"So I hear."

They drew closer, coming in for a kiss. Her lips tingled with the anticipation of it.

But then he paused, a tingle away.

"You hear that?" he whispered.

And she did. Bells pealing, choruses caroling.

The sound of cars outside ruining it all.

He kissed her anyway, letting her know that nothing was going to stop them.

Not even the Coles versus the Thomsens.

PRESSING HIS MOUTH TO HERS—so warm, so moist—he felt like the luckiest damned guy in the world.

She wanted to grow with him, to stay with him.

He sipped at her lower lip, pulling at it as he disengaged; it slid out of his mouth, sinuously, lazily.

Then he softly kissed her one more time, holding her face in his hands as he kept his mouth lightly on hers.

"Ready?" he asked, the sounds of slamming doors just outside.

She smiled, her soft lips curving under his. "Let's do it."

He traced his fingers over her cheek before they both aimed for the door, hand-in-hand.

When he opened it to exit onto the porch, seven members of the warring families were already out of their cars, standing behind their vehicles as if using them as barricades.

On one side—Juliana's aunt Katrina and two uncles.

On the other—Tristan's mom helping Gramps to a stand while a couple of cousins backed them up.

Tristan squeezed Juliana's hand. "You knew you'd find us here," he said to the small crowd. "Too predictable, huh? And where are the rest of you?"

Before anyone else could talk, his mom shot him a glance of apology. "Someone called the sheriff back at the community center, and everyone—including Chad—stayed behind to help calm the situation."

Gramps clearly was beyond all that. In fact, Tristan could barely stand to look at him, because the older man seemed as if his heart was breaking.

"What's going on, Tristan, son?" he asked softly, leaning against the 1957 Ford Fairlaine Tristan had once restored for him.

The car seemed to be the only thing keeping him up, and for a moment, Tristan almost went to him.

But he knew that he needed to stay up here, with Juliana.

Luckily, his mom supported Gramps, and Tristan looked at her in thanks. She watched him, and he thought that, maybe, she was trying to share as much strength with her son as she had already given the older man.

"I'm in love with Juliana, Gramps," he said, simply, directly, but, in a way, it felt like a shout. A big, wonderful, uncontained shout. "I have been for a long time, and when we ran into each other over in Japan, we couldn't deny it anymore."

Gramps kept looking at Tristan. What was he thinking? Why wasn't he saying anything?

Then Juliana's aunt Katrina, a woman with sprightly, flyaway gray hair and a stout figure covered by a sun-flower-print dress, spoke up.

"Juliana," she said in a voice that sounded sweet, patient and schoolmatronly. "Is this why that family ended up with the painting?"

Juliana's hand tightened in his.

"Aunt Katrina," she said, "I hope you're not insinuating that I purposely let Tristan outbid me."

Her aunt sighed, resting a hand on her chest, closing her eyes as if she were having an anxiety attack.

This time, Tristan did start forward, fearing for the woman.

But then one of the uncles—Gary—touched her shoulder and shook his head, as if saying, *Now's not the time.*

An ally?

Vaguely, Tristan remembered how, once, there'd been talk of one of his aunts and Gary Thomsen, but nothing had come of it. Just rumors that had disappeared with the next juicy story in town.

Now he wondered if Gary and Aunt Joan had been cowed by the feud.

Wondered how many people had been caught in the middle and been too afraid to step forward.

But he didn't have much time to think about it before Aunt Katrina removed her hand and blushed, healthy as a horse again.

Caught.

Next to him, Juliana sighed in apparent relief. One of Aunt Katrina's legendary, convenient anxiety moments. But this was the woman who'd taken in Juliana as a daughter, so he couldn't fault her for much.

Except for everything they'd all been swept up in over the years.

Juliana was talking now. "Have you all come here because Tristan and I are the new painting now that the old one is out of play? We're not your reason to renew this feud—history's going to stop repeating itself right here and now."

"Juliana," Aunt Katrina said, shooting a glare to Gramps and his lot. "It's time to get in the car. He's a Cole."

As Gramps stayed quiet, the Cole cousins took affront to that, hurling a few choice accusations in return and starting all mouths to yapping again.

Dammit, these people. They didn't get it, and it saddened Tristan that maybe they never would.

Juliana's voice rang out over everyone else's, and the conviction in her tone went right to the center of him.

"I'm not going anywhere, Aunt Katrina."

There'd been a time when he'd believed that she would never give in to what was so obviously between them, but here she was, standing up for him.

Tristan Cole.

No one outside the family had ever done that before.

And when she slipped her arm around his waist, he pulled her in close, her sweet scent lulling him. The tempo of his body rhythms picked up as he thought about how they were going to be alone again when this tiff was over.

How they had all the time in the world now that they had nothing to hide anymore.

Now both families were staring at him and Juliana as if they were stubborn kids who were going to learn better.

Sure.

"Over in Japan," he said, "Juliana and I worked a lot

out, and I'm not just talking about personally. For the first time in years for both of our families, we sat down like reasonable people and actually communicated. Oddly enough, it even worked."

"Quite well," she repeated, but the subtler meaning was targeted at only him.

He tamed a smile. "We exchanged Emelie's and Terrence's writings, too, just to get some perspective."

Both sides of the family got worked up about that, and the tension thickened again.

"That painting we were all after," Tristan said, raising his voice, "was about pride, and it's about time we all let go of it."

The Cole cousins shook their heads while Gramps remained still.

"Never," Aunt Katrina echoed.

Juliana took her turn. "Maybe you all should look at what Terrence and Emelie wrote, too, because none of it makes sense unless you see where the other was coming from." She looked up at Tristan. "They loved each other more than anything, and if they saw how everyone was acting now, generations later, they'd be absolutely sick."

As the group started to grumble again, Tristan ignored them, instead glancing down at Juliana and losing himself in her gaze—a future of dreamscape colors.

Then he turned toward his grandfather.

"Gramps," he said, "I love you. But is this how you want people to remember you?"

The older man peered up, and Tristan could've sworn he was getting to him.

He addressed the others. "And the same goes for you.

Do you want to be a footnote of this feud or is there something more worthwhile you could do with the rest of your lives?"

That stunned them, but the younger feuders started to backtalk Tristan, as if they were defending the feud out of habit.

Suddenly, he could see how the bitterness had survived, how it had turned over from year to year.

Juliana pressed her face against his chest, as if that could make this all go away, and he held her closer.

He could tell that she'd had enough, that they'd done all they could do until they could face their own families in private and try to talk some sense into them.

Standing on her tiptoes, she gave him a tiny kiss on the jaw, then said against his skin, "Be right back."

It was tough to let her go just when he'd gotten used to holding her, but he did. And as she headed for Aunt Katrina, he realized what she had in mind and, in turn, he went straight for Gramps.

"If you want to continue this skirmish with our visitors," he said mildly as he reached the hood of the car, feet away from the rest of his family, "I'd be grateful if you'd take it to the main house, not here."

Gramps was the most stubborn, most old-school man Tristan knew, but when he looked at his grandson, he'd lost all of that.

"Why do I have the feeling that I have no choice, Tristan?" he asked. "That you're already gone?"

He reached out, put his hand on his gramps's thin shoulder. It had carried a lot over the years, even Tristan himself, back in the days when his grandfather had been strong enough to give him rides that had made Tristan feel on top of the world.

"Gramps," he said, "it's up to you whether I go anywhere."

Tristan's mom glanced at her son, her eyes holding a sheen. He knew she was remembering what it felt like to be so in love.

When Gramps didn't say another word—only opened the car door and wearily sat inside—Tristan's mom spoke.

"Your dad would bust his buttons right now," she whispered, then leaned over to kiss him on the cheek.

She got into the car, too, along with the cousins, who kept giving Tristan dirty looks.

But Gramps?

He gazed out the window at Tristan, even as a cousin pulled the car out and then down the driveway.

By this time, Juliana had persuaded her own relatives to leave, too, and as they motored away, she watched them, her hands on her hips, the ends of her hair stirring in the whipped-up breeze.

Just looking at her, Tristan's emotions spun into their own dervish, then settled in him—his heart, his *life*—rearranging everything from the inside out.

"That wasn't so hard," he said.

"Aunt Katrina said she'd talk to me over dinner." She paused. "But I think she knows that she could lose me over this, and she's just as horrified by that as I am."

"My gramps got the same message, too. We'll see what that means now, I guess."

Juliana started to walk over to him, and his heart picked up speed. "They'll make the right decision. Won't they?"

Even though he didn't have an answer, she nestled her hand in his.

Her touch sent warmth through his fingers, up and over the rest of him, as they walked to the porch then sat in the glider to watch the last of the dust settle back to the ground.

JULIANA CUDDLED against Tristan on the glider. "My aunt Katrina promised they'd go straight home. No more shenanigans with the painting. At least not today."

"Thank God for that."

Juliana paused, thoughtful. Like her, Aunt Katrina had always possessed a soft side, stocking the bookstore with the biggest romance section within a fifty-mile radius and reading every novel from cover to cover. With Tristan's permission, she wanted to show Terrence's journal pages to her aunt. Maybe it would help.

And maybe not.

They'd just have to see, but whatever their families' attitudes, it wasn't going to take Juliana from Tristan's side ever again.

He laughed, suddenly and deeply.

"What?" she asked.

He pulled her closer. "Just thinking that we made a pretty good team."

"We did, didn't we?"

She rubbed her nose against his neck, slid her hand over his stomach. His muscles jerked under her fingertips.

His response sent a spike of desire right down the middle of her, and she shivered.

"Since we're all about wiping the slates clean," she said, "I apologize for being so difficult."

"Don't."

"No, I really should." She traveled her fingers up his chest, fidgeting with a button. "Until today, you were the one who had enough guts to come out with what we felt for one another. I didn't."

"Well, I don't have to live with Aunt Katrina's fake anxiety attacks." He coaxed his finger underneath her chin and guided her gaze to his. "Besides, you ended up coming out like a warrior."

The next thing she knew, he was kissing her, long, soft and hard all at once.

It seemed to last for hours, with them sipping and drawing at each other, with her sliding a leg onto his lap so they could get even nearer to each other.

She gave herself over to the sensations—to *him*—completely, going pliant in his arms as the outside breezes warmed them.

Outside, she thought. For anyone to see.

Then he did something that rocked her: he sucked her upper lip into his mouth and ran his tongue along the inside of it.

She jumped, just as if she'd been zapped between the legs.

He laughed softly, then kept stroking her with his tongue.

It felt as if she were being lifted off the glider, into the air as the ache in her turned into sharp, compressed agony.

He used his tongue to stroke her again, and with a thrust of daggered need, she went wet, nearing an explosion.

Panting, she clung to him, and he took that as his cue

to scoop her into his arms, right off the glider. He held her tightly to compensate for the fact that she'd gone down-right buttery.

"Yeah," he said. "I think things are going to go pretty smoothly after all."

He carried her toward the front door, looking into her eyes the whole way.

"But what if I still turn out to be a lot of work?" she asked.

"I love to work you."

All she heard was the word *love,* and it ricocheted all around her.

"I love it, too," she said. "But not as much as I love you, danger boy."

Smiling and whispering, "I love you, too," he brought her inside, kicking the door shut on the rest of the world.

Epilogue

WEEKS LATER, Tristan was going through some boxes he'd stored in a closet in his cabin years ago. Some of them had belonged to his dad, but he'd never been able to open them until now.

He hadn't wanted to catch the scent of his dad's clothes and see old pictures, but Juliana, who was helping him move to a big apartment in town where they would both live, was making this a far less excruciating experience than he'd imagined.

At the moment, she was asking questions about his dad's high-school photos, in one of which he was posing next to a flame-painted hot rod.

"Is this where you get your vintage-car genes?" she asked. "From Papa Cole?"

Tristan nodded, wiping at a dirt smudge on her face. It made her look just so cute—like an idealized Dickens street urchin—that he thought better about cleaning it all the way off.

"I caught the fever from him, all right." He dug some books out of his box. "He used to court my mom in that souped-up vehicle. He said she'd squeal when he sped around the country lanes."

"I can imagine your mom having the time of her life."

Juliana and his mother had bonded quickly. In fact, she was doing pretty well with the rest of his family, too, even Gramps, who'd read Terrence's and Emelie's writings and realized the extent of what they'd lost…and what Gramps didn't want the grandson he loved so dearly to lose.

Tristan looked up toward the wall in the other room, where he could see *Dream Rising,* perched there because Gramps had thought it might be a decent gesture.

An opening for two families who were working on ironing out their differences and uniting.

Aunt Katrina had been here the day they'd hung the watercolor, and she and Gramps had even gone so far as to share a meal with Tristan's mom and the new couple.

But it hadn't been very hard to persuade Katrina after she'd read Terrence's side of the story and realized, too, that Juliana wasn't going to surrender Tristan.

The rest of the family had followed their lead, even though there was still the odd dust-up from the younger ones every now and then. It'd be a while until everyone could fully swallow their pride, yet there was definite hope that they'd all settle matters some day.

As Juliana continued exploring the pictures, Tristan went through the books, using a work towel to wipe them down.

What did they have here? A collected work of American literature from the 1800s.

A volume of Southern California history.

And…

Tristan inspected a slim book with tattered binding wrapped in plastic. He opened it to find handwritten words on brittle, yellowed pages.

"Well, damn me," Tristan said.

At his surprised tone, Juliana scooted over to him, gasping when she saw the state of the book, too.

Tristan read the first page, then stopped. "Another journal of Terrence's. I've never seen this one before."

"Why don't you read it while I finish with some of these boxes," she said, leaving him alone.

But not before she ran her fingers over his cheek. Maybe he had a cute dirt smudge, too, but from the affectionate look on her face, he thought the gesture came more from her heart than from wanting to clean him off.

"But—"

"Go ahead." She smiled. "Take some time with him."

She kissed his cheek, then carried one of the boxes outside, where she would load it into his pickup.

As he began to read—quickly and eagerly—he was barely aware of Juliana continuing to work around him.

Over an hour later, he was done, and he extended an arm to her, summoning her over.

Her eyes were wide with curiosity and maybe even a feeling that Terrence's journal would drop a bombshell, so Tristan put her mind at ease right away.

"I don't know why my dad kept this particular journal to himself—there are no big secrets, nothing mindblowing. Maybe it was just lost among all his books."

Juliana motioned to the boxes they'd pulled out of storage. "Not an impossibility. What was in the journal?"

"Mostly reflections on Emelie. Terrence wrote this when he got sick—tuberculosis. It ended up leading to his death, and he must've known it was the end of the road when he started this book."

"Sad."

He nodded, his words scraping out of him. "There's one part though…"

She was so attuned to him by now that she knew what to do, smoothing back his hair tenderly, making his throat go even tighter with heat.

"What part?" she asked.

"He and Emelie hadn't seen each other for years after she married Klaus Thomsen, and he built her that house on the property where Aunt Katrina and some of the others live now."

The old place had burned down fifty years ago, but pictures of it were amazing. Klaus had gotten rich with a gold strike, and by the time he met Emelie, he'd worked his money into a fortune.

"They never ran into each other much," Tristan added, imagining how Emelie might have spent her days looking out one of the windows across town, in the direction of the Cole ranch, where Terrence lived. Tristan had done the same with Juliana once. "But one day, when she attended a daughter's wedding at the church on Main Street, Terrence came face-to-face with her. Both had grandchildren with them."

Juliana rested her hand on the back of his neck. "Both of them must've aged a lot by then. I wonder if they ever wondered what it might've been like to grow old together."

"Terrence did. But most importantly, he'd forgiven her for taking the painting by that time. His sourness about *Dream Rising* had turned to longing, and he thought she felt the same way when their gazes caught as they passed each other."

"They didn't even stop." Not a question.

"No, they didn't." He took Juliana's hand and held it. "She didn't reveal anything about still loving him—even if she did until the day she died. So he didn't say a word as they walked off in opposite directions. The painting was lost, and so was any chance that either of them might have had with each other."

Silence arched between them, but Juliana wrestled it back down. "Isn't it a good thing then," she asked, her voice quivering slightly, "that we didn't pass each other by like they did?"

"Yeah," he said, enveloping her in his arms, breathing her in and knowing he'd never let her go. "It's a good thing."

While they held each other, he closed the worn book, letting go of the past.

Claiming the future.

"I love you, Thomsen," he said.

"And I love you, Cole," she answered, taking the journal from him and putting it aside.

* * * * *

Don't miss the first installment in the exciting new
Special Edition continuity

THE FOLEYS AND THE McCORDS

Melanie Grandy is a girl with secrets, looking for a fresh start. And working as a nanny for powerful Texas tycoon Zane Foley seems like the perfect path to a new life. Until she falls for her sexy boss and his adorable little girl. But will the CEO return her feelings when he learns the truth about her past?

Look for
THE TEXAS BILLIONAIRE'S BRIDE,
by Crystal Green.
On sale July 2009
wherever Silhouette books are sold.

*Celebrate 60 years of pure reading
pleasure with Harlequin®!*

*Harlequin Presents® is proud to introduce
its gripping new miniseries,*
THE ROYAL HOUSE OF KAREDES.
*An exquisite coronation diamond, split as a symbol of a
warring royal family's feud, is missing! But whoever
reunites the diamond halves will rule all....*

*Welcome to eight brand-new titles that unfold
to reveal the stories of kings and queens,
princes and princesses torn apart by pride and power,
but finally reunited by love.*

Step into the world of Karedes with
BILLIONAIRE PRINCE, PREGNANT MISTRESS.
*Available July 2009
from Harlequin Presents®.*

Alexandros Karedes, snow dusting the shoulders of his leather jacket and glittering like jewels in his dark hair, stood at the door. Maria felt the blood drain from her head.

"Good evening, Ms. Santos."

His voice was as she remembered it. Deep. Husky. Perfect English, but with the faintest hint of a Greek accent. And cold, as cold as it had been that awful morning she would never forget, when he'd accused her of horrible things, called her terrible names....

"Aren't you going to ask me in?"

She fought for composure. Last time they'd faced each other, they'd been on his turf. Now they were on hers. She was in command here, and that meant everything.

"There's a sign on the door downstairs," she said, her tone every bit as frigid as his. "It says, 'No soliciting or vagrants.'"

His lips drew back in a wolfish grin. "Very amusing."

"What do you want, Prince Alexandros?"

A tight smile eased across his mouth and it killed her that even now, knowing he was a vicious, arrogant man, she couldn't help but notice what a handsome mouth it was. Chiseled. Generous. Beautiful, like the rest of him, which made him living proof that beauty could, indeed, be only skin deep.

"Such formality, Maria. You were hardly so proper the last time we were together."

She knew his choice of words was deliberate. She felt her face heat; she couldn't help that but she damned well didn't have to let him lure her into a verbal sparring match.

"I'll ask you once more, your highness. What do you want?"

"Ask me in and I'll tell you."

"I have no intention of asking you in. Tell me why you're here or don't. It's your choice, just as it will be my choice to shut the door in your face."

He laughed. It infuriated her but she could hardly blame him. He was tall—six-two, six-three—and though he stood with one shoulder leaning against the door frame, hands tucked casually into the pockets of the jacket, his pose was deceptive. He was strong, with the leanly muscled body of a well-trained athlete.

She remembered his body with painful clarity. The feel of him under her hands. The power of him moving over her. The taste of him on her tongue.

Suddenly, he straightened, his laughter gone. "I have not come this distance to stand in your doorway," he said coldly, "and I am not going to leave until I am ready to do so. I suggest you stand aside and stop behaving like a petulant child."

A petulant child? Was that what he thought? This man who had spent hours making love to her and had then accused her of—of trading her body for profit?

Except it had not been love, it had been sex. And the sooner she got rid of him, the better.

She let go of the doorknob and stepped aside. "You have five minutes."

He strolled past her, bringing cold air and the scent of the night with him. She swung toward him, arms folded. He reached past her, pushed the door closed, then folded his arms, too. She wanted to open the door again but she'd be damned if she was going to get into a who's-in-charge-here argument with him. She was in charge, and he would surely see a tussle over the ground rules as a sign of weakness.

Instead, she looked past him at the big clock above her work table.

"Ten seconds gone," she said briskly. "You're wasting time, your highness."

"What I have to say will take longer than five minutes."

"Then you'll just have to learn to economize. More than five minutes, I'll call the police."

Instantly, his hand was wrapped around her wrist. He tugged her toward him, his dark-chocolate eyes almost black with anger.

"You do that and I'll tell every tabloid shark I can contact about how Maria Santos tried to buy a five-hundred-thousand-dollar commission by seducing a prince." He smiled thinly. "They'll lap it up."

* * * * *

What will it take for this billionaire prince to realize he's falling in love with his mistress…?
Look for
BILLIONAIRE PRINCE, PREGNANT MISTRESS
by Sandra Marton
Available July 2009 from Harlequin Presents®.

We'll be spotlighting a different series every month
throughout 2009 to celebrate our 60th anniversary.

Look for Harlequin® Presents in July!

TWO CROWNS, TWO ISLANDS, ONE LEGACY

A royal family, torn apart by pride and its lust for
power, reunited by purity and passion

Step into the world of Karedes
beginning this July with

BILLIONAIRE PRINCE, PREGNANT MISTRESS
by
Sandra Marton

Eight volumes to collect and treasure!

REQUEST YOUR FREE BOOKS!

2 FREE NOVELS
PLUS 2
FREE GIFTS!

HARLEQUIN®

Blaze

Red-hot reads!

HB09R3

High rollers, high stakes
and a killer fashion sense.

Three sexy new mysteries from

STEPHANIE
BOND

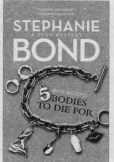

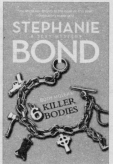

April 2009   May 2009   June 2009

"Bond keeps the pace frantic, the plot tight
and the laughs light."
—*Publishers Weekly*, starred review,
on *Body Movers: 2 Bodies for the Price of 1*

In 2009 Harlequin celebrates
60 years of pure reading pleasure!

We're marking this occasion by offering
16 **FREE** full books to download and read.

Visit
www.HarlequinCelebrates.com

to choose from a variety of
great romance stories
that are absolutely **FREE!**

(Total approximate retail value of $60)

We invite you to visit and share the Web site
with your friends, family
and anyone who enjoys reading.

You're invited to join our Tell Harlequin Reader Panel!

By joining our new reader panel you will:

- Receive Harlequin® books—they are FREE and yours to keep with no obligation to purchase anything!
- Participate in fun online surveys
- Exchange opinions and ideas with women just like you
- Have a say in our new book ideas and help us publish the best in women's fiction

In addition, you will have a chance to win great prizes and receive special gifts! See Web site for details. Some conditions apply. Space is limited.

To join, visit us at
www.TellHarlequin.com.

COMING NEXT MONTH
Available June 30, 2009

#477 ENDLESS SUMMER Julie Kenner, Karen Anders, Jill Monroe
Three surfer chicks + three hot guys = one endless summer. The Maui beaches
will never be the same after these couples hit the waves and live their sexiest
dreams to the fullest!

#478 HARD TO RESIST Samantha Hunter
American Heroes
Sexy, straight-as-an-arrow Texas Ranger Jarod Wyatt is awestruck by the
New York skyline and the stunning photographer snapping his portrait. As soon
as Lacey Graham spies the hunk through her lens she knows she has to have
him…even if she has to commit a crime to get the good cop's attention!

#479 MAKE ME YOURS Betina Krahn
Blaze Historicals
Mariah Eller was only trying to save her inn from being trashed. So how did she
manage to attract the unwanted—and erotic—attention of the Prince of Wales?
Not that being desired by royalty is bad—except Mariah much prefers
Jack St. Lawrence, the prince's sexy best friend....

#480 TWIN SEDUCTION Cara Summers
The Wrong Bed: Again and Again
Jordan Ware is in over her head. According to her late mother's will, she has
to trade places with a twin sister she didn't know she had. She thinks it will be
tricky, but possible…until she finds herself in bed with her twin's fiancé.

#481 THE SOLDIER Rhonda Nelson
Uniformly Hot!
Army Ranger Adam McPherson is back home, thanks to a roadside bomb that
cost him part of his leg. But he's not out yet. He's been offered a position in the
Special Forces once he's back on his feet. The problem? His childhood nemesis
seems determined to keep him off his feet—and in her bed....

#482 THE MIGHTY QUINNS: TEAGUE Kate Hoffmann
Quinns Down Under
Romeo and Juliet, Outback-style. Teague Quinn has loved Haley Fraser since
they were both kids. But time and feuding families got in the way. Now Teague
and Haley are both back home—and back in bed! Can they make first love last
the second time around?